AFTER THE
STORMS

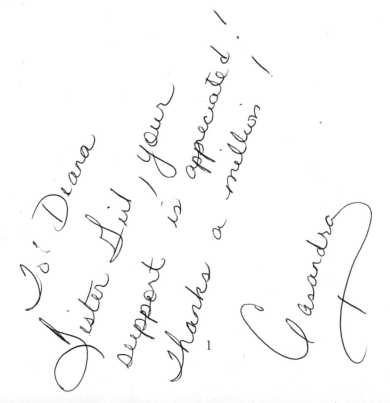

1

AFTER THE STORMS

Casandra Belcher Tripp

Casandra Belcher Tripp

DEDICATION

(My span of thanks goes to many, but all of you know who you are, but just to name a few....)

This book is dedicated to my daughter Rondericka Tripp for always telling me, you can do it Mama.

To my three men Israel, Isaiah and Judah Tripp for the love, smiles and memories you give me daily. I see the best in you!

To the three of the strongest women that ever lived, who made sure I'd make it, Laura Elizabeth Dixon, Mary Jane Hardy and Brenda Delois Bullock, thank you. Each of you taught me that I could anything! I know you see me doing what I always dreamed I do.

To John Henry Gray, my uncle, my most unpredictable relative. When I think of you, I think of me. One never knows what we'll do or say, and for that I love you.

To my late uncle, Rev. Dr. Clarence Bernard Gray Sr., whom I recently lost, I just want to say thank you for being my spiritual father. You didn't always see me in services, but I know you kept me in prayer! No matter how often I delayed the pursuit of my passion; you never let me forget that with God, I could do anything but fail.

To my aunts and uncles who have gone to be with the Lord, I love you for all the memories, we've had. You taught me how to love, cook, fight, listen, stand up for myself and to be a woman of virtue.

THANK YOU !

ACKNOWLEDGEMENTS

YOU MAY NOT SEE YOUR NAME, BUT YOU KNOW WHAT YOU DID!

I would like to first thank my Lord and savior for enabling me to do what I do.

I would also like to thank my family for standing by my side through thick and thin. Just knowing that you're a call away has made my life a joy.

To my brothers, sisters, cousins and friends, where would I be without you? I honestly do not want to think about the answer to that. Just know that **I LOVE YOU!**

A special thank you goes to those who make sure I have all that I need on a daily basis. Reginald Barrett, I want to thank you for not killing me when I call you at three in the morning. Thank you Celebrity Stylist, William "Big Willy" May, for making sure that my hair is always in place, when I do as you tell me (inside joke).

Minister Sylvia Barnes, Rabbi Alysa Stanton and Rev. Dr. William J. Barber, II, I thank you for the words of encouragement and support that you've given me through the years.

My New Visions Writers Family and A Sister's Expression Book Club Members, from the bottom of my heart, your support has made the difference. It is with great and abundant joy that I inform you that you will never be forgotten.

I can already see the faces of my nieces as you read this. I have not forgotten you. Your time is coming. There are so many of you that I am going to wait until 2014 and acknowledge you. You too are loved, and will never be forgotten.

To my coworkers I know you wonder some days, but I want you to know I appreciate your support. You listen to me rant, you attend my events, you support me financially, you read my material, you make sure that I stay grounded, and because of you, I can do what I do best, be creative.

Jacquelin Thomas, Sandy Dowd, Suzette Perkins, Titus Pollard, Monique Miller, Angela January, Karen Brown, Trice Hickman, Michelle Bowen, Ella Curry, Sharvette Mitchell, Yolanda Gore and all of the others in the industry that have helped me along the way.

To the awesome editor, Carla Dean who took extra time out of her life despite many challenges and made it happen, I just want to thank you again!

To Dashawn at Hot Book Covers, you just did your thing!

To my readers, I want to **THANK YOU** for supporting me by purchasing my book and my desire is that you send me e mails and share your thoughts with me. Again, I thank you!

Table Of Contents

Casandra Belcher Tripp

Weathering The Storms Of Life

Trees swayed, branches bowed, and trash cans filled with debris rolled into the streets while rain poured from the dismal gray sky as Hurricane Josephine headed for the town of Turner. The moisture on the windows made it virtually impossible to see outside. As the wind whistled, dogs and wolves howled like never before.

September seemed to be the month for trouble in this small, rural South Carolina town. For the last one hundred years, or as far back as people could remember, the history of tragedy in the town of Turner seemed to have dampened the spirits of the residents. Just last year, we thought the September troubles had bypassed Turner. Yet, low and behold, on the last day of the month minutes before the stroke of midnight, a family of five was killed in a mysterious house fire.

I sat in my modest office sorting paperwork, reviewing files, returning telephone calls, praying, and occasionally glancing out of the window at the wind and rain. I took a few seconds to listen to The Weather Channel. The meteorologist was in the middle of giving the latest Josephine updates when I closed the Porter file after careful review. Knowing that in eleven hours a hurricane could possibly be approaching frightened me.

How can something so powerful destroy so much and hurt so many? I thought to myself.

Mr. Kyle Carroll yelled as he broke through the glass door and slammed it shut, sending shards of flying glass all over the place. He slammed it with such force that the door was mutilated.

The sound of shattering glass stunned me. Before I knew what was happening, a hurricane had touched down right in my office. My chest began to tighten, and my breathing became erratic. I could taste my own blood. Hurricane Kyle had hit first, a day ahead of schedule.

"Miller, why aren't the Sutton and Porter files in the file room?" he asked in a harsh tone.

Kyle Carroll was all of five feet, six inches tall and weighed about three hundred pounds. He was unmarried and in his early sixties. His thinning red hair along with his burly eyebrows went with his tomato red face and sour disposition. His round, protruding belly resembled that of a potbelly stove. His high-water slacks and white socks were hideous.

"I have the files right here," I said, looking up at him. "I was reviewing them prior to the merger. I needed to concentrate and the file room was crowded," I offered as humbly as I could. "The file clerk knew which files I had and when I'd be returning them."

With his hands placed on his pudgy waist and a scowl on his face, he interrupted me.

"You know it's against company policy for files to be removed from the file room without your immediate supervisor's approval. I want to see you in my office…now," he said sternly, then turned and hobbled away as if his run-over black shoes had been set ablaze.

"He 'bout to be crazy," I said under my breath as I jumped out of the chair and trailed after him.

Despite the fact that I weighed right at two hundred pounds, even in a rage of anger, I moved with both speed and elegance. My black shoulder-length hair swayed freely about my shoulders, while my prominent dimples were still evident despite my anticipation of the confrontation that was sure to come.

"I can surely tell time by that man. He's gonna make me go off one day," I said to myself as I headed to his office, while attempting to avoid the tiny fragments of glass, as well as the obvious stares from inquisitive co-workers. I began to say a silent prayer.

"Sheretta Miller, you know the policy. I'm writing you up," he shouted.

Mr. Carroll moved to his chair and flopped down. I took a seat opposite him as he grabbed an ink pen, a disciplinary referral, and began to write.

"I don't like your attitude. You're a bad example for the other employees here at WeCumm."

While sitting in the chocolate leather chair facing the cluttered mahogany desk that housed one angry, unreasonable individual, I refrained from letting my emotions run rampant with the speed of a wild cheetah.

"I have worked at WeCumm Communications for over fourteen years. I was here before you, and I've never been written up. The reason I took the files back to my office was to make certain the accounts were in order. I am well aware of the policy. I am also aware of the fact that the merger is about to take place, and the Sutton and Porter accounts are two of our largest open accounts."

Ignoring me, he pushed the white disciplinary referral in my direction. "Sign here," he said flatly, then reached over and pointed to the employee signature line as if I couldn't read.

"I will sign it because of the company policy. I am also writing a handwritten note next to my signature," I stated as I wrote. "Is there anything else before I return to my office?"

"No," he snarled between clinched teeth.

My fury was like never before as I left his office. I just made it inside the confines of my office before totally losing control. I sat behind my desk trembling uncontrollably, trying to regain my composure as salty tears poured down my cheeks. Tears and rage blurred my vision. I knew it was time to take action; I'd put up with his shenanigans for the last time. I had the exterior of Hercules, but my heart was as soft as melted butter, and my true countenance was that of Cinderella.

13

"This is my job and I have to do what's right, even if he is a pain in the behind," I said to myself.

As I peered out the window, I noticed the wind and rain had eased off just a bit. Tree limbs, leaves, slithers of paper, and other foreign objects covered the ground. With all of my might, I tried to concentrate on my daily duties and make sure I maintained my professionalism while doing my job in an exemplary manner. Still, my next plan of action was heavy on my mind. I knew I had to provide documentation that would save my reputation, and at the same time, I had to follow the WeCumm employee grievance policy guidelines.

My next move would be a meeting with Ms. Hardy, the Human Resources Specialist for WeCumm Communications. Although she was not well liked, it was a known fact she was fair, firm, and consistent. Ms. Hardy was always neat; however, the clothes she wore were better suited for a woman twice her age. She'd been with WeCumm for over ten years and was in her late thirties. It was rumored she had become a prude because of two failed marriages.

My wrath lingered, causing the day to speed by. I'd been able to get all of my daily tasks done. I'd even started on tomorrow's work, and it was only four o'clock. I still had an hour left before my day would officially come to an end.

"I forgot to eat," I mumbled as I popped a lemon drop in my mouth.

I'd been so busy working that my appetite had faded. I picked up the copy of the referral rebuttal, a pen, and a legal pad. I whispered as I began to write. *Dear Ms. Hardy....*

Samantha stood in my doorway and asked, "Hey, Sheretta, are you alright?"

Samantha Sharpe was nosey, but she also had experienced her share of unpleasant incidents with Mr. Carroll, and because of that, she was well aware of the ruthless person he was capable of being.

"I saw him demolish your door, and I prayed you wouldn't get up and take him out. Girlfriend, you kept your cool."

Samantha was a hard worker. She always came on time and left on time, as well. In addition, she was the office gossiper.

"I had to keep my cool, or else everybody at WeCumm would have been evacuated from the building by now," I joked.

"I know that's right," Samantha said, while heading for the elevator. "This weather is rough. I'm going to get some batteries, bread, milk, water, and make my way home. I'll be in bed by the time the hurricane hits."

She refused to work overtime after Mr. Carroll wrote her up for submitting two hours of overtime, when at the last minute, he'd asked her to complete a report he needed for the Board of Directors meeting.

On the way out, I noticed Ms. Hardy coming out of her office with her red leather bag on her shoulder. She was tall, and a pink floral-print blouse and pair of beige pull-on slacks adorned her plus-sized frame. Word in the office was, she was anything but approachable, but I had to try. Fate, opportunity, and whatever had presented itself.

"Excuse me, Ms. Hardy. I have a quick question for you. I know you're trying to go home and get out of this weather. So, I promise I won't take up too much of your time."

"Sheretta Miller from accounting, right?" she asked, flashing a friendly smile.

"Yes. I was wondering if you'd be able to see me tomorrow. I would like to submit an attachment to my disciplinary referral."

Her eyes narrowed as she spoke. "I haven't seen a disciplinary referral on you."

Ms. Hardy then turned the key in the lock and jiggled the knob to make sure the door to her office was locked.

She nodded her head, offered a smile, and added, "I'm sure my processing assistant has the referral but just hasn't had an opportunity to scan it into the system and forward it to me." In an instant, thunder cracked the sky and the building shook. "We'll talk about it tomorrow, if Josephine spares us. Those clouds are thick, black, ugly, and I have got to go." She looked past me toward the double windows at the end of the hall.

My mind ventured to another planet as I drove through the flooded streets, only stopping at red lights and stop signs. My windshield wipers began to stick; I could barely see the cars ahead. From what I could see, traffic was moving at a snail's pace because of an accident. As the sirens whizzed by, I searched for Monroe's patrol car.

While passing the grocery store, I noticed the crowded parking lot. There did not appear to be one empty parking space to be had.

"Thank God for allowing me to plan ahead," I said as I bypassed the stores, acknowledging the fact that I'd purchased my storm staples three days in advance.

After entering the side door leading into the kitchen, a vase of fresh flowers that hugged the counter caught me by surprise. I took a deep breath, smiled, and walked over to the granite counter to read the card attached to the cardholder nestled in the arrangement. The aroma of the pink roses filled the room. The flowers accented the spring green décor in my rustic kitchen. The oval wrought-iron pot rack, which hung over the oven island situated in the center of the spacious kitchen, often served as a conversation piece for my guests.

I headed upstairs to my bedroom. My queen-size bed occupied only a portion of my sleeping quarters. The bright red comforter accented with cream and the matching curtains had been a gift from my grandmother just before her sudden death. Whenever in my bedroom, I often thought of her.

As I peeled off my damp black slacks and pink blouse, I placed them across the laundry hamper to dry and then headed for the shower. I knew Turner would be one of the first municipalities in the area to lose power. When the power outage did occur, I wanted to be settled in. In 1999, Hurricane Floyd left us without power and water for five days.

After a relaxing shower with my favorite body wash, I slipped on pajamas and went downstairs to my formal living room. It was the area closest to the door if I needed to evacuate due to the storm.

I cuddled up on my chocolate sectional sofa with my Bible, laptop, two flashlights, an unopened bottle of vitamin water, my mason jar of pink lemonade and ice, a bowl of beef fried rice, and my cell phone. I read my favorite scripture while taking slow sips of my pink lemonade. I had two pages typed in less than ten minutes. My mind as well as my notes were cooperating tonight. My rebuttal would be thorough. Once and for all, Kyle Carroll would be exposed for the arrogant tyrant he was. He'd been mean and cruel to many, but I wasn't about to stand for his mess anymore. I had documented the facts, plain and simple – the unadulterated truth.

All of a sudden, the ringing of my cell phone brought me back to reality. Looking at the screen of my Droid, I knew who was calling.

"Hello," I responded with cheer, my heart rate quickening. "Thanks for the beautiful roses."

"Hey, you've seen your surprise. So, obviously, you're safe and sound inside."

The chuckle coming from the voice on the other end of the phone was enough to make me smile. The baritone voice of Monroe, my beau of two years, always seemed to excite me. Monroe was one of Turner's finest.

"Is there anything you need?" he asked.

This call was confirmation that I was sure to spend another stormy night alone. The sound of rain beating down on my rooftop, mixed with whipping winds, gave me an eerie feeling and, once again, sent my heart racing. "Yes, I'm safe and sound. Where are you?" I inquired, already knowing the answer to my question.

I knew he was dedicated to his job, and he took the safety of the citizens of Turner serious. Therefore, he was somewhere in town on patrol.

"It would be nice if we could watch a movie and share a bowl of popcorn from time to time, and thank you for asking. I have everything I need. I went to the grocery store days ago. You know I hate last-minute shopping."

"I wish I could be there, but I'm patrolling the south side. We've had some reports of flickering power and several elderly residents live in this neighborhood. I've already knocked on the doors of the elderly residents that I knew had no family in the area, just to make sure they were safe and had the supplies they needed," Monroe stated between radio calls and static. "The chief assigned me to this area. Besides, Grandma Tate lives here. I should have known you were prepared."

"Such a gentleman, and a handsome one at that," I taunted. "I hope you know that I'm really proud of you." The crackling sound of limbs sent shivers of fear through my body. "I'll be praying for you."

"Don't make me blush. I love you, and as always, I thank you for your prayers," he chirped before ending the call.

In his own way, Monroe was handsome. My attraction to him manifested when I first laid eyes on him. He spoke with authority, yet his firm demeanor was transparent. He was average in height and had a stocky build. His huge black eyes were like magnets. His pecan-colored skin was flawless except for the half-inch scar on his left cheek. He wore his coarse black hair in a close cut, and boy was he a sharp dresser—both on and off duty.

Being a native of Turner, he knew everyone in the area, even Mr. Kyle Carroll. Knowing Monroe was protective when it came to me, I said nothing about the happenings of the day. If I had, there would surely have been drama at WeCumm Communications LLC come daylight.

During the early morning hours, we were recipients of some good news. We were relieved to hear that Josephine had weakened overnight. Once again, we'd been spared a September tragedy thus far. All we could do was pray the last twelve days of the month would remain uneventful. During the course of the night, I managed to capture only four hours of sleep on my sofa. The wind and rain continued to pound on my rooftop throughout the night, waking me occasionally.

As I sat at my kitchen table, I took slow slips of my coffee. I thought long and hard about the days ahead. My cell phone began to ring.

Recognizing the ringtone, I pressed my earpiece and said, "Good morning, Officer Tate."

A groggy, "Good morning. How are you?" he responded.

The background noise from the radio was loud and clear.

"Wow, you sound rough," I said, while rinsing out my coffee cup and placing it in the dishwasher.

I went to the freezer in search of something for dinner. I placed a package of chicken in the sink to thaw.

"Thanks for the compliment," he continued. "You sound lovely. I just wanted to let you know I'm logging off for the day. I'll see you this afternoon for dinner and a movie at your place. Have a good day at work."

I knew I couldn't let him know just what was going on at work for more than one reason.

19

With cheer, I said, "I will, and remember, get some rest. I'll see you tonight."

As I ended the call, I took a deep breath and prayed that everything would be all right.

I was usually the last person to arrive at work, but this morning, I was ten minutes early, only to witness additional degrading comments from Kyle Carroll.

"You are stupid," yelled Mr. Carroll. "Why is that wet floor sign not in the maintenance room? It should not be in the middle of the hall. You are incompetent."

"Sir, I apologize," Mr. Curtis McCall, our custodian, pleaded. "I'm sorry, sir. I didn't want anyone to slip coming in from out of the weather and all," he said, looking at Mr. Carroll with weary light brown eyes.

He had a smooth medium brown complexion and a receding hairline. He'd worked at WeCumm for over thirty years. His frail body was as thin as a rail. All he ever did was smile and lend a helping hand when needed.

"Mr. Carroll, I was only trying to do my job."

I stood out of Mr. Carroll's view and made sure I took careful mental notes on the happenings of his latest attack. Mr. Curtis was a deacon at Mount Pisgah, and unless a demon had taken over his body during the storm, he would never act out of character.

"In my office now!" Mr. Carroll screamed at Mr. Curtis, while walking in the direction of his stale, cluttered office.

As Samantha passed me on the way to the lounge, she whispered, "Mr. Curtis is the victim of the day."

She often wore an excessive amount of makeup, but today, she'd obviously applied enough for two days.

"Unfortunately, thank God it wasn't me," I responded.

As I made my way inside my office, I whispered a prayer that Mr. Curtis would stay calm and not feed into Mr. Carroll's outburst of the day. After working on some accounts, I looked at my watch and noticed it was almost time for my meeting with Ms. Hardy. I picked up the folder to leave my office and noticed Samantha talking on her cell phone.

Thank goodness, she's on the phone. I can make a clean getaway without answering any questions about my intended destination, I thought.

My brown rubber rain boots were slick. I'd just missed the fall of my life as I entered the lobby of the Human Resource complex. I grabbed the back of a nearby chair just in the nick of time. I regained my balance and caught my breath before taking another step.

"Hello, I'm here to see Ms. Hardy," I said to the elderly brunette who wore bright red lipstick and sat behind the circular reception station loaded with family photos.

"She told me that she was expecting you," she responded as she looked up at me. Then she smiled, turned to the side, and pointed in the direction of Ms. Hardy's office. "You may go right in."

"Thank you."

With the blue file folder in my right hand, I walked toward the rear where Ms. Hardy's office was located.

"Good morning. We made it through another storm. Let's just hope the remainder of September is safe for all of the citizens of Turner," Ms. Hardy greeted with a reserved smile on her banana complexion face. "Please have a seat."

"Yes, we did make it through the storm. Did you get my referral?" I asked eagerly, my eyes glancing down at her tidy desk in search of the referral.

"No, and I asked my processing assistant if she'd seen it, but she said no."

"Several employees have been written up, and in conversation, none of us have received the notice from human resources that we should be given after a disciplinary write up. The treatment we often receive is unfair and humiliating. I've also noticed some discrepancies in a couple of the larger accounts. Could you please have a senior supervisor in central accounting look into them?"

"Yes, I will. Just what exactly do you think we should be looking for?" she asked.

Ms. Hardy wrinkled her forehead while her eyes studied me with the intensity of a brain surgeon in the operating room.

Looking in her eyes, I eased to the edge of my seat and said, "According to the revenue the accounts are bringing in, some of them should be in the corporate accounts division. I can't put my finger on it, but at least two of the accounts are being under billed according to my calculations and according to the services they're receiving. At the same time, they're not showing a profit for WeCumm, when in fact, they have all the signs of being revenue-producing accounts."

"Sheretta, please keep our conversation confidential until I contact you," Ms. Hardy said as she placed her burgundy pen in the holder on her desk.

"I have an eerie feeling something is not right. I've enclosed some of the information in my response. As you requested, I will keep our conversation confidential." I said, then placed the blue folder in her hands before leaving.

As I went back to my office, I thought about what Ms. Hardy said. Knowing I had made a promise to keep our discussion confidential, I avoided Samantha at all costs. Not only was she nosey, she had a way of finding out what she wanted to know.

It was almost five o'clock, and I was ready for an evening of relaxation. Monroe and I had a date to watch a movie at my place, and I needed some peace. So, I could not wait to get home.

"See you tomorrow," I said as I left the building.

Samantha and Mr. Curtis stood at the edge of her desk talking. In deep conversation, they both waved in my direction without even looking at me.

In less than twenty minutes after arriving home, I had chicken in the oven and a vegetable medley on the stove simmering in seasonings. Most of my dinner was on; all I had to do was prepare a packet of boil-in-bag rice, heat the rolls, and dinner would be done.

Upstairs, my bed was summoning me, but I knew I could not answer the call. After my shower and a body pampering session, I slipped on a pair of slacks, a blouse, and sprayed a light mist of my favorite body spray behind my ears and on my wrists. After tidying my bathroom, I was downstairs in less than an hour.

I lit some scented candles and began playing soft music from the latest romantic hits CD I'd ordered. Then I sat on the sofa and dozed off. A short while later, I woke up and scurried around to make sure everything was in place.

I went to the kitchen, put the rice on, and prepared the rolls for the oven. When the doorbell rang, I knew who would be standing on the other side. I took a glance in the brown-framed oval mirror in the narrow hall near the front entrance to make sure I looked good.

As I opened the door, I heard the oven timer beep. I stood and looked at him, the plush cream carpet enveloping my bare feet while the sight of him held me hostage. I saw the white roses in Monroe's hand. Remembering my oven alert made me move toward the kitchen.

Darting away with a smile on my face, I said, "Come on in. Dinner is just about ready. Thank you for the flowers. Please put them in the vase on the mantle," I said, then paused to admire him. "Flowers two days in a row? I must be special," I teased.

"You're welcome. Always remember, you are special to me. Dinner smells great!" He said as he walked in the living room. "How was your day?" he yelled over his shoulder while moving to the mantle.

"It was indeed a day. I was busy from the time I arrived to the time I left. It was as if every account holder wanted to speak to me directly."

I took a second look at Monroe. It was as if his khaki slacks and orange polo accented every muscle in his body.

"Baby, you know how to treat people, and they appreciate that. Every Sunday, you send Grandma Tate a hot meal if she doesn't feel like coming over after service. You don't have to do it, but you do." He rubbed my shoulder. "Can you tell me why you dislike red roses?"

"I do it because we were taught to always take care of our elders. You know as well as I do that when Grandma Tate was younger, she took care of the people of Turner. She was the midwife, the doctor, and the cook for anyone who needed her," I answered. "As far as red roses, I cannot tell you why I don't like them, but for some peculiar reason, they give me the creeps."

"You're right, and you are a caring person. That's why I love you so," said Monroe as he moved his hand down the side of his face. "And don't worry, baby. I'll never send red roses. You're my lady, so you can have whatever color roses you desire."

I looked up at Monroe and said, "Thank you."

"You're welcome. Now, I'm hungry. Let's eat."

Monroe gently took my hand and moved toward the dining room. He pulled my chair out, waited for me to sit, and then slid my chair under the table.

After grace, we fixed our plates from the mini table buffet I'd prepared. It was obvious Monroe and I were both famished. We finished dinner in less than thirty minutes.

"I think I'm going to have some chocolate for dessert," I told him, as I moved from the dining room table to the refrigerator where I stored my chocolates.

"I'm watching my weight. So, I think I'm going to pass, but by all means, help yourself."

"I will." I made my selections from the gold box. "Let's go to the living room. I'll put the dishes in the dishwasher a little later."

Monroe sat on the sofa and I tossed him the remote control.

"When are you going back on the firing range with me again?" he asked.

Easing down beside him, I replied, "I appreciate your gift, but I'm just not comfortable firing a gun."

Then I nuzzled closer to him with hopes that he'd forget the subject.

"Just let me know when you're ready. You need to know how to protect yourself."

I figured we were both aging, because in less than a half hour, the movie was watching us. I woke up with my eyes looking upward at the chandelier and the vaulted ceiling.

After we were both awake and coherent, we said our good nights. After he left, I went into the kitchen to place the dishes in the dishwasher and checked to make sure all of the candles had been blown out. Again, I could hear my bed calling my name. This time, I was in no position to argue. I gave in without so much as a fight.

Days passed, allowing me the opportunity to continue searching through accounts, not to mention keeping an eye on the actions of Kyle Carroll. To no surprise, his actions remained the same. I did my best to stay out of his way because I didn't know if I could handle another one of his attacks.

Finally, Friday arrived, and Mr. Carroll picked a new target—Tony from the copy room. Little did he know, but Tony was the wrong person to attack physically or verbally. Tony was a Desert Storm veteran who stood over six feet tall, weighed more than three hundred pounds, and had muscles galore. He worked hard and kept to himself. He'd only been with WeCumm a little over three years, but he'd never missed a single day of work. In the midst of Mr. Carroll's attack, Tony put all of the bystanders in shock. We each held our breath as we waited for what we all knew would be Kyle Carroll's last stand. However, to the surprise of the entire east wing of WeCumm Communications, Tony stayed calm, nodded his head, and remained silent. He then went into the copy room, closed the door, and left each of us standing in awe, including Mr. Carroll.

Mr. Carroll looked at us out the corner of his eye. He turned his head in a swift movement, only to see everyone staring at him. He had no choice but to cut the tongue lashing short since he'd been left standing in the middle of the floor looking like a clown who had just been left behind by his circus family. It was obvious Tony had gotten the best of him by walking away.

The co-workers were in a huddle whispering. My telephone took my attention from the disturbance outside my door, as well as the gathering of the others who'd heard the racket. Having a glassless door enabled me to hear the conversations from my office.

"Sheretta, Ms. Hardy would like to see you in her office," her receptionist said.

"Okay, I'll be there shortly," I told her just before placing the phone in the cradle.

I took my coffee cup to serve as a distraction. I knew Samantha would inquire as to where I was going if I left my office with a folder in my hand heading in the direction of the Human Resource complex.

After rounding the corner, I stopped in the lounge and put my coffee cup in the cabinet.

When I walked in, the receptionist was on the telephone. She motioned me to Ms. Hardy's office with a hand gesture and a smile. I could see that Ms. Hardy's door was open.

"Hello. Please take a seat," she said, extending her arm and directing me to the black leather chair across from her desk. "First of all, I cannot discuss personnel issues, because as I'm sure you know, it is against company policy. You have done a superior job, and you've been here almost fifteen years. However, I do want to offer you a new position as the Accounting Supervisor for commercial accounts..."

I interrupted her mid-sentence. "That's Mr. Carroll's title. So you're telling me there will be two accounting supervisors for commercial accounts?" I paused. "I don't know how that will work. Mr. Carroll is not the easiest person to work with," I added with a sigh.

"Again, I can't disclose any information, but I can tell you that your tips were accurate. Central Accounting reviewed several accounts, and disputes were found. I don't think you'll have to worry about him." She pressed her lips together and nodded her head. "We will begin a massive audit next Monday."

My mouth dropped, and before I knew it, I said, "I'll take it."

"Congratulations are in order. My processing assistant will contact you Monday morning in order to begin your paperwork."

I sprang from my seat and turned to leave, but stopped. "Thank you, Ms. Hardy. I appreciate the opportunity."

On my way back to my office, all I was able to say was, "Thank you, Lord. Thank you, Lord." My journey back was indeed a joy. When I reached the end of the hall, I remembered I didn't stop to get my coffee cup. Before I could turn and go back to get it, I heard a commotion coming from my hall. Looking up,

I saw a group of people in a huddle staring in the vicinity of Mr. Carroll's office. I followed the direction of their stares only to see the security team in there. My eyes expanded and my breathing became irregular.

With wobbly legs, I went into my office and propped myself against the filing cabinet. I peeked as the coworkers stared at him packing his things. The crowd gathered stood and watched as they escorted him out of the building with a cardboard box in hand. While being marched out, he gazed at me through the glassless door. As he peered at me, he seemed to slow his pace, and then he resumed at his regular gait. It was as if his eyes were speaking. The entire east wing stood and stared at him as he was removed from the building.

When they were gone, I took a seat at my desk. The east wing was abuzz. I took a few minutes and thought long and hard about the storms I'd weathered in my life. I knew by the grace of God, I could make it.

In The Midst Of The Storms

I'd been watching television in the dark and must have fallen asleep. I saw a shadow as I sat up on the sofa. I knew I had to retrieve my weapon to protect myself.

"I've got to end his life so I can live in peace."

Boom! Boom! Gunfire and flashes of light pierced the air. The hair on the back of my neck and arms stood at attention. The potent odor of the shotgun powder burned my nostrils. Having gnawed my bottom lip with a vengeance caused blood to drip. The taste of blood gave me a surge of energy and a boost of confidence. After pulling the trigger, I realized I'd missed my target.

I shook like a tree leaf on a windy day. Warm fluids streamed down my numb legs. My designer outfit was now an unimportant factor. Rain, urine, and mud now soiled my suit.

Boom!

Power, fear, and tension clouded my judgment as I squeezed the cold trigger with closed eyes. Time was crucial if I was to survive this ordeal.

A variety of blue-gray hues roamed the sky. Streaks of lightening zigzagged from the sky to the earth. Rain covered me from my head to my bare feet. The temperature had dropped, causing my feet to stick to the earth. Chestnut coloring from my hair dripped onto my blouse and suit collar.

The thunder roared as if it were a mighty lion.

This man has to be blown away. This man has to be blown away right now. I've gotta do it. Goodbye, I thought. Taking precise steps in his direction while blinking away tears and rain, I raised my hands and took my stance. My left foot was planted firmly on the ground as I aimed the shotgun at his head.

Monroe's face was crystal clear. I could see the scar on his left cheek as he lay on the ground next to the tree trying to pull himself up. It was as if he were sending a message with his eyes. They were petitioning for a second chance at life.

Tears trickled down my face. I loved him with all my heart, but this I had to do. It was either him or me.

Monroe had somehow pulled himself up.

I bent my trigger finger and squeezed.

Boom! Boom!

Monroe's body thumped down on a bed of leaves and twigs. Blood oozed from his head and abdomen.

Startled by a loud bang, I woke.

"Help me," I screamed, sitting straight up on the chocolate sectional while pulling the blanket to cover my stomach.

Hugging myself, I took deep breaths and shook my head, trying to erase the nightmare from my psyche. My eyes darted from left to right at the speed of a missile as I trembled.

Jumping to my feet, I sprinted to the kitchen and snatched my cell phone from my designer bag. Hearing Monroe's voice was all that mattered.

"Hello, beautiful," he said immediately after answering.

Panting, I said, "Thank God you're okay."

"What's wrong, Sheretta?" Monroe uttered. "Are you okay?"

Unable to speak, I gasped in order to breathe.

"What's wrong?" Monroe asked again. "Where are you?"

"I'm home. Of course, I'm okay," I lied.

"I'm scheduled to clock out in a few minutes. You sound strange. I'm on my way."

The shrieking sound of his siren snapped me out of my daze.

"No, that's not necessary. I'm fine. I had a bad dream, that's all."

"Are you sure?"

"Yes. I fell asleep when I came in from work. This has been an unusual day."

"If you say so."

I could no longer hear the sound of Monroe's siren.

"Well, since I fell asleep, there will be no home cooked meal this Friday."

"You act like that's a surprise. We always go to dinner on Friday when I'm not working overtime or private duty," Monroe stated. "Wear jeans. I feel like a casual Friday."

"Oh, I forgot," I chuckled. "Jeans are cool. Besides, I have some new jeans I've been waiting to wear. By the way, I've got some news for you," I said with little emotion before finishing one statement and continuing with the next.

"What's going on?" Monroe asked.

"It's a secret. The look on your face will be priceless when you hear my news."

"That's not fair. If that was me withholding a secret, your lips would be stuck out from here to south of the border."

"I've got a beep. I'll see you when you get here," I told him, then switched calls. "Hello. Helloooooo. Hellooooo."

After a pause and no response, I pressed the end call button, placed my phone on the granite countertop, and went to the stainless steel refrigerator to retrieve a bottle of water. After taking a sip, I shook my head and shrugged my shoulders while leaning on the counter.

"My cell phone is acting crazy," I mumbled to myself. "It must be because of the recent storm. Earlier today, when I pulled into the garage, my phone rang once and then stopped."

I knew we would be going to dinner, which meant there would be no meal for me to prepare. A gander at the clock on the microwave displayed the time as 6:39 p.m.

It had been a long day. I took the steps one at a time instead of the usual two. I sat on the edge of my queen-size bed. The picture of Monroe that sat on my nightstand seemed to have a different appearance than ever before. It was as if his eyes were seeking answers. Despite the fact he wore his uniform, he seemed powerless in the photo.

"What are you trying to tell me?" I said just above a whisper. "First the dream, now the picture."

Monroe would arrive in less than thirty minutes. So, a quick shower would have to suffice. He was usually off at five, but this day, it was obvious something kept him at work later than usual.

From my upstairs bedroom window, the September breeze placed me in a solemn state. The trees moved front to back, left to right. The wind seemed to be going in a circular motion, the pattern of a dance move. Debris from the recent storm was still visible. Rain droplets hit the window ten by ten. In seconds, the droplets ceased, and my mind seemed to return to the present.

Monroe's house was minutes from my condo. Knowing he was prompt was all that was needed to get me moving. A shower and body treatment later, I had squeezed into my new jeans, a gold sweater, my butter hiking boots, and was now ready to take on the town of Turner and one handsome Monroe Tate.

When the doorbell sounded, I knew who to expect. Monroe graced me with his presence right on cue.

Just before opening the door, I took a peek in the mirror.

"Perfect," I said after pressing my lips together to even my lip moisturizer.

"Hi, baby." He strolled past me, but not before placing a tender kiss on my lips. "So...are you going to tell me about your priceless news?"

His jeans accented his perfect buttocks. The black leather blazer, charcoal gray designer shirt with hints of black and purple, accompanied by his cowboy boots gave him a look of total distinction. My eyes and nostrils expanded with a whiff of his cologne. I looked in his eyes again and realized just how handsome he was.

"I have a new position. I got a promotion today," I squealed as I pressed my palms together, placed my fingertips to my lips, and smiled.

"Congratulations. What? When? How?" he rattled on, while looking at me with wrinkles in his forehead and narrowing his eyes.

"Mr. Carroll was terminated, and I was promoted. Everything happened so fast. I'll fill you in at dinner," I chirped.

"What? How'd that happen?" Monroe asked with squinted eyes and a tilted head.

"If you can't wait, I'll tell you all about it on the way."

I removed my jacket from the coat rack and shoved it in his hands. Monroe held the jacket as I slipped my arms into each sleeve. After stepping outside, he twisted the doorknob to make sure it was locked. The brisk air made me shiver. The hair on the back of my neck spiked as if the presence of evil was lurking nearby.

After closing my door and going to the driver's side, he climbed in. Once he buckled his seatbelt, he looked at me and said, "I'm waiting."

"During the past few months, I suspected that Mr. Carroll has been involved in some unethical business practices," I said matter-of-factly, while buckling my seatbelt. "After noticing some fraudulent activity where some of our larger accounts were concerned, because at least three of them were my accounts, I was afraid the blame for mishandling them would fall on me," I told him, then paused.

"Go ahead. I'm all ears."

I continued. "He'd been mean, rude, and vindictive. Several people in the department, including me, had been having some personnel issues late—"

Monroe interrupted me. "So you mean to tell me that he'd been messing with you, and you hadn't told me?" he asked through clenched teeth, his nostrils flaring.

"I knew how you'd react, so I tried to handle things on my own."

I saw Monroe's grip on the steering wheel tighten and his jaw line become firm.

"Sheretta, why are you just telling me this?" he growled, then slammed on the brakes and honked at a dog that was lounging in the street.

"Because I knew you'd hit the roof first, then Kyle Carroll second."

"I'm disappointed that you'd think I couldn't handle myself. I'm an officer of the law for God's sake," he uttered. He gnawed on the inside of his jaw and made a sharp left. "I think we will stay close to home to-night. I have an early morning tomorrow. What about Turner's Café?" he asked.

"That sounds good to me. The drive is always a well-needed change of scenery, as well as a deviation of the faces we're accustomed to seeing, but I'm glad we're staying close to home. I want to do some cleaning this weekend. I can get an early start in the morning."

"Okay," Monroe responded flatly.

The radio and Monroe's uneven breathing pattern were the only audible noises heard during the somber six-block drive.

Turner's Café was known for the family atmosphere as well as handmade burgers, homemade soups, tasty sandwiches, and specialty desserts. The beefy vegetable beef soup and turkey, bacon, and cheese sandwiches always seemed to hit the spot when I'd frequented Turner's Café for lunch. Dinner at Turner's Café would be a definite change from our usual Friday dinner outing in Charleston.

The green and red neon sign in front of the rectangular-shaped brick building filled the picture window and lit the dark night. Upon our entrance, we were met with aromas of different foods, while the chatter of patrons filled the quaint space known as one of the family friendly hangouts in the small town. Three huge ceiling fans with cherry wood blades seemed to shine a bit brighter by night, while the black, white, and burgundy floor glistened. The eight booths that lined the walls were separated by the glass-front door, which served as the main entrance. Each of the six round tables was covered with plastic burgundy and white plaid tablecloths. Silver rectangular napkin holders, salt and pepper shakers, and ketchup sat on each booth table and on the circular island. The country decor provided a relaxed atmosphere, while delivering the picturesque view they were accustomed to.

"Hey, how y'all doing?" greeted the slender waitress with a southern twang as she made her way to the last booth, carrying a tray of food that smelled delicious. She wore a white blouse and black slacks, which was the uniform for this establishment.

"Hi," we said in unison.

"Hi, Officer Tate," said a boy who sat with his parents at a booth to the left of the door.

Monroe acknowledged the boy who appeared to be between nine or ten years of age.

"Hello, Israel. How are you doing in school this year?"

He displayed a million-dollar smile. "I've been doing great so far."

"Well, you take it easy. I'll see you when we begin our DARE Program next month."

"I will. See you later, Officer Tate."

Monroe nodded at the youngster's parents as we walked away.

"That was Deacon Curtis McCall's son, daughter-in-law, and grandson," I noted. "They left Mount Pisgah to join Deliverance Temple."

"Israel was one of my brightest students in the DARE Program last year. I knew I hadn't seen them at Mount Pisgah in a while."

We made our way to the outer portion of the circular island, which housed eight burgundy leather bar stools in front of the cooking station manned by three uniformed individuals in white tops, black bottoms, and long white aprons. Monroe always made it a practice never to sit with his back to an exit. He slid onto one of the bar stools after I'd taken my seat. Couples and families had filled Turner's Café on Friday and Saturday nights for the past twenty years.

After climbing on the chrome pedestal barstool, I placed my handbag on the empty barstool to my right and took a look at the menu.

Monroe picked up his menu and glanced over it in absolute silence.

"What looks good to you?" I asked amidst the conversations going on by other café occupants.

Out of nowhere, a baby squealed, bringing the peaceful atmosphere to a halt. I caught a glimpse of a figure outside the café gazing inside looking in our direction. As heads turned to see why the baby was crying, I was able to see the shadow of the person. When I attempted to make eye contact, the individual turned and darted out of my view.

I whispered, "Maybe that wasn't him."

"Did you say something?" Monroe asked.

"No. I was just thinking out loud," I lied.

"I think I want a bowl of beefy vegetable beef soup and a turkey sandwich with honey mustard, lettuce, tomatoes, and red onions," he said as he placed the menu on the counter, never looking in my direction.

"I'll have a ham sandwich with provolone, lettuce, and light mayonnaise, and a bowl of Cajun chicken noodle soup, please," I said, then laid the menu on the counter and looked at Monroe. "You sure are quiet tonight."

"Just thinking." He paused, turned his head in my direction, and looked into my eyes before continuing. "Well, I worked late, and you've had a busy day," Monroe said as he stole a glance at me. "Besides, you're watching your weight, and Turner's offers a heart healthy menu."

"I might be watching my weight, but according to the struggle I had getting into these jeans, I'm not doing a very good job of it," I remarked.

"You look terrific to me."

"Aren't you the charmer tonight?" I said.

"You know I call it like I see it," Monroe stated as he sprinkled pepper from the clear shaker with the silver top.

"Flattery will get you a free meal. Dinner is my treat."

"Thank you."

After a quiet meal, I paid our bill, and we headed to the parking lot.

"Dinner in town was a nice change," I admitted, looking at Monroe.

We were at my condo in no time at all.

Monroe cut the engine, removed his seatbelt, turned at an angle, looked in my eyes, and spoke. "Sheretta, I want you to promise that you'll never keep a secret from me again."

His baritone voice soothed me.

"Monroe, I was only trying to protect you."

He held my hand in a tight grasp. "I'll protect you for as long as I live, but you've got to promise me that you will never keep secrets from me again."

"I'm sorry, Monroe. I promise."

As tears streamed down my cheeks, he wiped them away, one by one, while placing gentle kisses on my forehead.

"By the way, you look good to me," he said, then pulled me closer and joined his lips to mine.

The evening breeze stirred my senses. It contained a distinct smell, a mixture of sweet rain in addition to another ingredient that I couldn't identify. As he walked me inside, each step became slower than the one before. He removed his leather coat and hung it on the coat rack. Then he stood motionless and stared into space.

Monroe finally took a seat on the sectional and asked, "Have you had a chance to get the new CD by Brother Gibson?"

"Actually, it's in the player."

Monroe stood and moved to the entertainment center to retrieve the remote. He returned to the sofa before pressing the play button. I nestled under his arm, laying my head on his chest.

"I'll be in Beaufort working undercover for a few hours tomorrow," Monroe said as he looked down at me. "We're leaving at ten in the morning."

"Will you be back for church Sunday?"

"I sure will. This is a routine sting. We're going to arrest some bad guys." He paused. "I'm hoping to return in time to help you prepare dinner. I'll call you on my way back." He yawned as he laid his head on the back of the sofa. "Remember, I won't have access to my cell phone, so I'll call you."

"Wake up, sleepyhead," I taunted, noticing we'd been asleep about an hour.

"I guess it's time for me to turn in. The music was listening to us snore. I'll call you the minute I see the Turner city limit sign."

We made slow strides to the door. Twice, Monroe stopped, turned to look at me, and kissed the back of my right hand. He shook his head, picked up his pace, and moved toward the door.

"Goodnight," I said.

Again, he came to a halt. "Sheretta, please promise me that you'll never keep secrets from me again. I love you, and it's my job to protect you."

"I promise. I know how defensive you get when it comes to Grandma Tate and me. I didn't want you to lose your temper and beat the daylights out of Kyle Carroll."

After a tender kiss, he turned to leave. When he reached the bottom step, he turned and opened his mouth as if he wanted to say something, but instead, he blew me a kiss.

"What a restless night," I said, pulling the covers up to my chin.

I literally tossed and turned all night. The morning sun was unusually bright for a September day. Looking at the clock on my nightstand was a reminder that Monroe was working undercover. I couldn't call him for the usual words of comfort he provided on the mornings after sleepless nights.

My first order of business was to shower, dress, and head to Wal-Mart before the crowd began to occupy every square inch of the store. The parking lot was evidence that I'd missed the mark.

"Hello, Sister Sheretta," I heard a voice call out as I turned on the cookie aisle, only to look up and see Reverend Walters' smiling face.

"Good morning, Reverend Walters. I see you're trying to beat the crowd, as well."

"Sister Sheretta, I thought I was early. According to the checkout lines, I'm not." He chortled while shaking his head. "Let me get going. I'll see you, Mother Tate, and Officer Tate in service tomorrow, as usual." He confirmed his own statement with a nod.

"Yes, sir, we'll be there with bells on."

"Bless you," Reverend Walters said, then pushed his cart down the aisle out of sight.

Reverend T. J. Walters, the pastor at Mount Pisgah Baptist Church stood right at six feet tall and had a heart of gold. In his thirteen years as pastor with us, there hadn't been so much as a rumor of infidelity or wrongdoing. He was a loving husband, father, and a man of integrity. His striking looks and wheat complexion, accompanied with hazel eyes, often raised the eyebrows of women in the congregation and the community, but he always managed to remain scandal free.

"Where has the time gone?" I asked myself as I drove out the antique shop driveway.

I'd searched high and low for the perfect table to place the statue of the African warrior that had been a gift from grandmother's mission trip to Africa. Grandma always told me that one day I'd marry a strong warrior, and until that day, she'd leave a warrior to watch over me.

A flip of my right wrist indicated it was well after four. Grabbing my cell phone from my bag, I sent Monroe a text and began Sunday dinner.

My hands were immersed in water, cabbage, and salt. My cell phone rang half through the cleaning process. I flung my hands, grabbed a towel to dry them, and pressed the Bluetooth button to answer the call.

"Monroe, what took you so long to call me back?" I murmured while patting my hands with the towel. "It's about time you called."

There was no response.

"Hellooooo."

Still no answer, but this time, I could hear shallow breathing on the line. I pressed the Bluetooth button to end the call, leaned on the sink, and took a look at my cell phone. The call had come from an unknown number. I knew when Monroe was out in the field, he didn't want me to call, but something on the inside insisted that I call him. So, I dialed his number, only to get his voicemail on the first ring. My hands trembled and my heart pounded.

"His battery must be dead," I said loud enough to be heard as I stared into space.

The ringing of my landline ended my trance. I looked at the screen on the cordless, only to see Grandma Tate's number.

"Monroe's back. He went straight over to check on Grandma Tate. He's such a devoted grandson." I smiled as I picked up the cordless phone. "Hello. I was wondering when you were going to call me."

"Hello, Sheretta. Was I supposed to call you, baby?"

I immediately recognized the strong yet soft voice of Grandma Tate. "Hi, Grandma Tate. I thought you were Monroe," I answered with a bit of uncertainty.

"I was just calling to see if you'd heard from my Monroe. He said he'd be back before dark."

"His cell phone is dead. He should be back any minute," I told her. "As soon as he charges his battery, I'm sure he'll call you. In fact, I'll make sure he calls you real soon. Let me get finished washing the cabbage."

"Okay, baby. What are you cooking for dinner tomorrow?" she asked.

"Barbecue chicken, a pork roast, cabbage, rice, fresh butter beans, and sweet cornbread are on the menu."

"Mmmm. My Lord, that sounds good to me," she remarked. "What time will you and Monroe be picking me up for Sunday school in the morning?"

"Grandma Tate, we'll be there at nine sharp," I replied with a chuckle.

"Please be here by nine. I want to get to Sunday school early. Last Sunday, you two were late, and I missed my chance to read the scripture of the week," she said as she cleared her throat.

The sound of Grandma Tate's television seemed to be louder than her. That was my opportunity to end the call.

"Grandma Tate, I know you're watching the news, so I'm going to let you go."

"All right, baby. Don't forget to tell my Monroe to call me the instant he calls you back." She then hung up without so much as a goodbye.

The doorbell rang just as I placed the cordless handset back in its cradle. I dashed to the door, closed my left eye, and took a peep. There was no one there. Shaking my head, I made my way back to the kitchen.

With dinner on, I made my way to the living room, took a seat on the sofa, propped my feet up on the ottoman, and pulled the cover over my stomach. My eyelids felt as though someone was pulling them down.

A whiff of simmering onions would be the next thing to capture my attention. I leaped from the sofa and dashed into the kitchen. The pork roast was simmering in mushroom and onion gravy, while the barbecue chicken was now golden brown. After removing the chicken from the oven, I considered swiping a wing before covering it with foil, but instead, I settled for a granola bar.

"After church, all I'll need to do is cook rice and bake sweet cornbread."

Nine o'clock, still no word from Monroe. After a second attempt to contact Monroe only to get his voicemail, I left a message.

"Monroe, the least you could do is call me and let me know you're okay. Grandma Tate is worried about you, too." I

42

sucked my teeth and pressed the button on my Bluetooth to end the call.

As I paced the kitchen floor, my stomach began to churn. I had to find something to occupy my time. The waiting alone was about to drive me wild. Two and a half clean bathrooms and a dust-free living room later, I took a gander at the clock. My time to wait was completely out. I was officially turning into someone other than the normally rational person I was.

"Think, Sheretta. What are you supposed to do in the event of an on-duty emergency?" I asked myself. "I've got to call Monroe's immediate supervisor. Where's that number?" I looked in my kitchen junk drawer and found the captain's business card that housed the raised gold shield. "If I don't hear from Monroe by midnight, I'm calling the captain."

I picked up my cell phone and dialed Monroe's number once more. He answered on the first ring.

"Hello, baby," Monroe responded.

"*Hello, baby?* Is that all you can say?" I screamed. "You should have been back hours ago. Why didn't you call and let me know what was going on? I was three milliseconds away from calling your captain."

"What? You didn't call the captain, did you?" he snapped.

"No, but I was about to!" I shouted. "You said this was a routine sting."

"Honey, you know how it is. When you're in the field, anything can happen." He lowered his voice even more. "I promise. I'll be more thoughtful next time."

"You know I was worried," I sobbed. "Where are you now? I want to see you."

"I just stepped into my house," he whispered. "I'll see you bright and early in the morning. I promise."

"Okay, it's late. I'll see you in the morning," I retreated.

"Okay. Goodnight, Sheretta."

Monroe rang the doorbell around eight-fifteen. If I hadn't been downstairs, I wouldn't have heard it.

"Good morning. You look beautiful," he declared when I opened the door wearing my turquoise and purple dress with accenting purple jewelry and purple pumps.

"Thank you." I looked into his bloodshot eyes. "Are you feeling okay?"

"I'm just tired, but enough about me. What're we having for dinner?"

"Oh, just wait and see. You'll be satisfied. By the way, I almost didn't hear the doorbell. Do you mind taking a look at it one day next week?" I asked.

"Yes, anything for you."

I looked in his eyes and said, "You know I feel the same way."

Monroe pecked me on my cheek as I grabbed my wrap from the coat rack.

"We've got to hurry. Grandma Tate called me bright and early to make sure we'd be on time," he declared. "She went on and on about not missing another opportunity to read the scripture in Sunday school."

I giggled. "I know. She just happened to mention that last night when she called to check on you. As one of the founding members, as well as the oldest member of Mount Pisgah, Reverend Walters always asks her to read the Sunday school scripture."

We arrived early enough for Sunday school. The parking lot was filling fast. Heels were clanking on the pavement, women were in their finest, and the men were G Q sharp.

Deacon Curtis McCall and Mother McCall arrived just as we were entering the Walters Educational Building. Mother McCall dressed to the hilt each and every time she stepped out, and today was no different. She wore a white designer suit with gold embellishments. Her pumps and matching bag must have cost a pretty penny. Her white hat seemed to sit on her head at an angle that barely allowed her to see out of her right eye. She was petite in stature; her medium brown skin accented her dark brown marble-like eyes. Even at her age, her body was that of a thirty-year-old.

The children's wing was buzzing with over three dozen children. In the last two years, First Lady Walters had devoted much of her spare time working with the youth, both in church and the community.

Grandma Tate stood in front of the adult Sunday school class with the aid of her cane, her head held high as she stated, "The Sunday school scripture for today can be found in the book of Psalms, chapter one hundred seven, and the twenty ninth verse. It reads, 'He maketh the storm a calm so that the waves thereof are still'."

Mount Pisgah held over three hundred comfortably. This day, the regal red velour pews were occupied by only about three quarters of the regular attendees. Several families had moved their membership to Deliverance Temple. Slowly but surely, the members were finding their way back home.

Halfway into the sermon, Monroe's cell began to vibrate. His focus on the sermon deliberately became intent. The vibration almost shattered the oak pew to pieces. I gave him a blank stare that he never acknowledged.

While Reverend Walters continued with the morning message, my mind became saturated in his words as I searched my Bible to follow the verses he quoted, highlighting the sections I wanted to reread.

45

He stood behind the oak pulpit gripping one edge with his left hand and dabbing sweat from his brow with his right hand as he chanted with teary eyes. "In the midst of the storms, you must always remember four things. One is that storms come to strengthen us. Two is that we all go through storms in our lives. Three, storms can and will test your faith. Last but not least, if you focus on God when storms arise, you will be the victor according to His word."

The piano player was in sync. The members stood with raised arms, crying and praising God in their own way. Sister Daniels did a holy dance, while Mother Gray pranced with her hand on her hip. The deacons just gave Him the praise.

Reverend Walters moved from side to side shuffling his feet and then did a 360-degree turn. The piano player and organist continued to hit the right notes at the right time.

"I just want you to know, God knows all," he chanted. "He sees all, and He protects His own." Tears ran down his cheeks like that of a stream. "Remember, in the midst of your storms, God's got a blessing waiting for you."

He reached the bottom step with the cordless microphone. Tears streamed down his cheeks as he continued.

"Often, we can't see through the rain, but you must know that as children of the King, you will come through the storm." He froze; his hazel eyes seemed to come in contact with each person in the crowd of over two hundred. "Only if you allow His hands to remain on you," he continued.

There wasn't a dry eye in the sanctuary. The aisles were congested. Women, men, boys, and girls shouted, cried, and gave God praise. Mother McCall, who had taken her seat, leapt to her feet and began prancing back and forth in front of the mothers' section while waving her satin, lace-trimmed handkerchief in the air as if it were a flag and chanting praises to God. Grandma Tate and the other mothers were in an uproar, as well. Because of their age and physical limitations, some were limited to praising God from the pews, while some were all over the sanctuary.

In Reverend Walters' closing, he made a plea for his brothers and sisters to remember their outreach duties.

"While we have our health and strength, let us not forget our brothers and sisters who are less fortunate," said Reverend Walters just prior to the benediction.

As we walked to the parking lot, Deacon Curtis McCall came to the area where Monroe and I stood waiting for Grandma Tate as she said her goodbyes.

"Congratulations, Sister Sheretta."

I turned and glanced at him, narrowed my dark brown eyes, and asked. "Congratulations for what?"

"For reporting Mr. Carroll to human resources for embezzlement," he said as he looked down.

"Deacon McCall, I only told the truth. Mr. Carroll has not done the right thing, and he has to be punished for what he's done," I continued. "You know for a fact that he has been unkind to many of us at WeCumm."

"Yes, ma'am. Well, have a great Sunday. I'll see you tomorrow," he said, then rushed away.

"Monroe, Sheretta, babies, I think it's time to eat. My stomach is talking," Grandma Tate said while approaching us.

Monroe chuckled. "Let's go. I thought it was just me."

After arriving at my place, dinner was on the table in less than twenty minutes.

"Baby, you sure can cook," Grandma Tate said, wiping her fingers with a napkin. "Tastes just like my cooking before my eyesight decided to go on vacation," she chuckled.

"Grandma, you're right. Sheretta's cooking does remind me of yours," Monroe commented. "It's as if she's already a part of our family."

"Well, son, we're just waiting," she whispered as she reached over and patted Monroe's hand, then winked at me.

I sat in silence and looked from Monroe to Grandma Tate respectively in that order.

"Monroe, why don't you take Grandma Tate into the living room so she can relax," I suggested.

"Okay."

"Lord, I'm so full I'll be asleep in a few minutes," Grandma Tate teased as Monroe helped her up. "Sheretta, baby, the meal was delicious."

"Thanks, Grandma Tate," I said, while pushing my chair from the table.

I could hear them laughing and chatting from the kitchen.

As I entered the living room, I noticed Monroe preparing Grandma Tate for the ride home.

"Baby, dinner was great, as usual. I thank you for all you do for me." She lifted her arm so Monroe could assist her with her coat and scarf. "I need to get home and close my blinds before dark."

"Now you know you're welcome," I said before planting a kiss her on her cheek.

"Sheretta, I'll see you tomorrow. It's getting late," Monroe uttered. "Good night."

After a peck on the cheek, he turned to leave, but before walking out the door, he stopped and whispered, "I made an appointment for us to go to the firing range Thursday afternoon at six sharp."

"Goodnight. I'll see you Wednesday evening, Grandma Tate. Monroe, I'll see you tomorrow, and Thursday it is."

I'd slept four hours before being awakened by a loud noise coming from the street. I lay in bed and stared at the dark ceiling, unable to return to slumber mode. The excitement of the promotion had my mind spinning. So much was planned for my first day as an accounting supervisor; sleep was nowhere to be found.

While preparing to back out of the garage, I noticed a bit of daylight, only to discover a foot of open space at the bottom of the garage door, which caused me to halt and exit my sport utility vehicle. After careful examination of the garage, I assessed there'd been no sign of forced entry. Nothing appeared to be missing, so I continued on to work.

"I'll call Monroe and have him come by and check things out," I said while watching the garage door close completely before driving off.

The WeCumm parking lot was almost bare. A glance at my watch indicated I had arrived twenty-seven minutes earlier than usual. Upon entering the building, Mr. Curtis McCall was exiting the office that would become my new home.

"Good morning, Sheretta. I just cleaned your office, and the glass technician will be here before noon today to replace the glass door to your old office."

"Thank you, Deacon McCall...I mean, Mr. Curtis," I chuckled. "I've got to make sure I call you Mr. Curtis here at work."

"You're welcome, and again, congratulations."

The first things to catch my eye were the two dozen pink roses arranged in a huge crystal vase with greenery and baby's breath. The arrangement along with the vase made the stale, unattractive office look like an executive suite. The once cluttered mahogany desk had a different look. The spacious hutch was now noticeable. The office now appeared fresh and vibrant. The glow coming through the window seemed to hold promise.

"Lord, I thank you for favor. Who knew when I applied for a transfer, that you'd bless me with a promotion?" Tears trickled and my heartbeat doubled while my hands became damp. "Get yourself together, Sheretta. You've got a job to do," I said, then pulled out my phone to send Monroe a text thanking him for the breathtaking arrangement.

Within twenty minutes, my old office, which contained only a few personal items, was packed, and in less than thirty minutes, my move was official. My next task was my nine o'clock appointment to sign my new salary agreement in Human Resources.

To my surprise, Mr. West and Mr. Cummings were in Ms. Hardy's office when I arrived. They both stood, greeted me as I entered, and remained standing until I was seated. Mr. West sat with a solemn look on his face, while Mr. Cummings sported a fake smile. They were both in their early fifties and had been born into their illustrious positions.

"Sheretta, I'm sure you know Mr. West and Mr. Cummings," Ms. Hardy said as she looked from one to the other.

"Yes, ma'am," I managed to utter.

Ms. Hardy began, "The investigation on the recent happening at WeCumm is still in progress. We'd like you to keep any and all information you have gathered confidential until our internal investigation has been completed..."

Mr. Cummings interrupted her. "We want to personally inform each account holder of the billing discrepancy and offer a chance to make any and all necessary corrections."

All eyes were on me as I sat motionless. It was as if I was the guilty party.

"I do understand. I have not and will not discuss anything in reference to my findings," I assured them.

The men stood as Ms. Hardy began to speak. "Sheretta, thank you for your time. My receptionist has the new contract for you to sign."

I stood, as well. "I thank you for your time and the opportunity," I said before exiting her office.

"You're welcome," Ms. Hardy said as the men looked on.

After signing the new contract, I trekked back to my office where my real tasks began.

My cell phone alerted me to a text from Monroe, which read, *Remember the brakes on your truck are just about shot. Do not drive, I will pick you up from work and you can drive my vehicle and I will drive yours to the shop.*

I responded, *It's going great. I'll be ready at 5:15.*

With so much to do on my first day and not realizing it was nearing noon, my stomach began serving notice. *I'm overdue for my morning cup of hot chocolate,* I thought to myself. I slid my stocking feet from my flats to my heels, which I stored under my desk. Then I pushed back my chair, grabbed my coffee cup, and proceeded out of my office.

"Good morning, Samantha," I said while passing her cubicle.

"Hi," she mumbled, never looking up from the paperwork she was collating on her untidy desk.

There were employees from several departments in the lounge doing one thing or another.

"Congratulations. We're proud of you," one male employee remarked with a smile.

"You deserve it," said another as she looked over the rim of her glasses from the book she'd been reading.

With his head held high and a smile across his face, Tony said, "Sheretta I thank you for the many times I know you have prayed for me, despite the fact you've never said anything. I know you've prayed for me; I know it. You've been praying. I cannot count the days I came to work with my mind made up that it would be Kyle Carroll's last day." His head was now down, and I caught a glimpse of the tears as they fell from his honey brown eyes. "Just when I was ready to execute my plan, you'd either come in our presence or my mind would flash back to your kind smile," he whimpered.

"Tony, are you okay?" I asked, ushering him to a corner near the broom closet.

"I'm okay," he replied. He swiped his eyes with the white handkerchief he'd pulled from his back pocket. "Thank God," I said as I took him by the hand and lead a silent prayer. "Amen."

Tony pulled out a small pocket Bible with a permanent fold on a particular verse. Upon examining it, I saw the scripture was in Isaiah.

"Isaiah fifty-nine and fifty-eight reads, 'The way of peace they know not, and there is no justice or right in their goings. They have made them into crooked paths; whoever goes in them does not know peace'." Tears vanished and a smile washed over his face. "I know God; I have peace."

"Look at God," I told him.

"Thanks again," he said, then returned to the front of the lounge.

Mr. Curtis stood was in a huddle talking with coworkers. When he spotted me, he dropped his head and scampered out, causing the group to disperse.

I stood in awe containing my emotions before going to make a cup of hot chocolate. A flip of my wrist indicated I'd been gone from my office for ten minutes or so. *I've got calls to make, clients to contact, and memos to compile. Back to work I go.*

"Samantha, how has your day been thus far?" I asked, stopping and standing less than five feet away.

"Fine," she yelled, looking up with a scowl on her face. Her nose was fire red and her skin displayed red undertones.

With a tilted head, I looked in her eyes and asked, "Are you sure? Is something bothering you?"

She dropped her head, sucked her teeth, and snapped, "I'm sure."

I walked away at a turtle's pace but stopped a few feet away. I turned to look at Samantha, gripped my cup, and continued to my office.

"It is the last day of September. I should be prepared for anything today," I mumbled.

Shrugging my shoulders, I sat behind my desk and removed my heels, replacing them with flats. The message indicator prompted me to check my voicemail. I entered my password, picked up a pencil and memo pad, and transcribed the messages.

"Wow, my first day on the job and ten messages in less than fifteen minutes. My work is cut out for me." I inhaled deeply before dialing the number to return the first call.

"Good afternoon, Mr. Sorenson. This is Sheretta Miller from WeCumm Communications returning your call. How may I help you?"

"Sheretta, I've been out of town. My wife and I have been at our beach house, so I must admit I got a late start today," he chuckled.

"Mr. Sorenson, that's understandable. I trust you both had an enjoyable weekend," I replied as I pulled his account up on the computer and saw his was not one that had been compromised by Kyle Carroll.

"Trust me, we did. We spent quality time together," he continued. "I read your email, and congratulations are in order. I want to assure you that both of my hotel accounts will remain with WeCumm. You've been a jewel over the years. If there's anything I can do to assist you in your new position, don't hesitate to contact me," he said.

"Thank you for the vote of confidence, Mr. Sorenson."

He tittered, "Young lady, you've been an asset to WeCumm. My secretary is buzzing. Again, Sheretta, I support you. Have a great day."

He was gone before I could utter my appreciation.

After more phone calls, emails, and interviewing applicants to take my position, I noticed it was almost five o'clock. I knew if I weren't ready when Monroe arrived, I'd never hear the end of it.

The glass in the door had been replaced, and Mr. Curtis had cleaned my old office. The floor had been stripped, redone, and the white blinds had been replaced. One last look at my old office gave me a sense of sadness. I'd endured so much pain in my tenure in that office. I never wanted anyone to ever feel as I had in the past.

When I went to the lounge to rinse out my coffee cup, I noticed Samantha's cubicle was empty. I looked at the clock on the wall; it was three minutes after five. She always stayed until five after five gathering her belongings and making a cup of coffee for the road.

"She must not be feeling well today," I said. "I'll check on her tonight."

The halls were empty. The hair on the back of my neck rose and my body trembled. I darted back to my office to grab my bag and laptop so I could be outside when Monroe arrived. He was always punctual.

I sat on the concrete bench and pulled out a book I'd been reading. The anthology had been done by several of my favorite authors. Upon finishing the anthology, I realized the evening sky was darkening.

"Where's Monroe?" I asked after noticing it was almost six, just before I picked up my phone to call him.

After no success reaching him, I dropped my phone in my bag. As I stood, I saw the headlights of an unfamiliar dark car entering the parking lot. I scurried to my vehicle, hit the remote, pulled the door open, threw my belongings inside, and slid in with lightning speed. As the car approached, I noticed the dark tinted windows. The tint was so dark it had to be illegal in South Carolina. It stopped directly in front of me and revved the engine as if it was going to ram into me. I froze with my hands gripped on the steering wheel.

"Go!" was all I said as I turned the key, shifted into gear, turned the wheel to the right, and floored it.

As I looked in the rearview mirror, my hands trembled when I saw the lights from the vehicle, which was on my tail. I was going sixty-five in a thirty-five. The car trailing me had to be going close to sixty-five, because it was merely inches from my bumper.

"Lord, I need you now," I uttered as I maneuvered the steering wheel with one hand and used the other hand to reach into my handbag to retrieve my cell phone. "Lord have mercy," I begged aloud as if there was someone in the vehicle with me.

Upon digging unsuccessfully, my cell began to ring. It was then I noticed it had fallen out of my bag and onto the floor. I cast my eyes in the rearview mirror with hopes that the vehicle would no longer be closing in on me.

When I bent over to reach for my cell, my grip on the steering wheel slipped. I lost control and swerved into the path of an oncoming truck. The sound of blowing horns was all I heard. Blinding lights from the truck beaming in my eyes terrified me.

Screeching tires and the blowing of horns were embedded in my mind as I closed my eyes and swerved off the road into a rain-drenched patch of soil, plummeting into the side
of a woody, mud-filled ravine.

Raging Storms

Sirens and chatter accompanied by red, blue, and amber flashing lights awakened me. I quivered as I looked into the faces of several firefighters, some I'd never seen before. As they questioned me, I looked with uncertainty from one to the other, moving only my eyes. Stars lit the dark sky, as I lay helpless in my vehicle while they removed me from the mangled mess. The sound of crinkling metal and noise from the monstrosity used in the rescue was agonizing.

Due to the rugged terrain, the shift from my vehicle to the plastic backboard was a challenge; any error in the move could land me in the rain-drenched swamp below. Afraid to let go, I gripped the shirt of a firefighter, holding on for dear life. I felt as though they were going to tip me over.

I licked my lips, only to taste fresh blood. Tears flowed like a waterfall. The smell of gasoline caused my body to tense.

"Okay, Miss, we need to get you to the road so we can transport you to the hospital."

As the emergency medical technician spoke in a manner that eased my mind, she massaged my fingers until I no longer gripped the blue uniform shirt.

While they lifted me from what seemed like one hundred feet below, I gazed between the female emergency medical technician and the husky male firefighter to my left. Broken glass, leaves, twigs, brush, my handbag, and a shattered laptop were among the scattered items visible as I cast my eyes between the five men and a lady. Despite their efforts to be gentle, I felt like I was in the spin cycle of an antique washing machine. Seconds after we were on level ground, a small explosion rocked the earth. The sound of flying objects as they connected with the ground, along with the hustle of the firemen as they extinguished the blaze, could be heard loud and clear.

"Sheretta, please open your eyes and listen," I heard a familiar voice say in a rushed manner.

Through teary eyes, Deacon Curtis McCall's soiled, tattered clothing and smudge-filled face were visible as I lay on the stiff board. My neck was in a brace; I was unable to move. My mouth was as dry as field cotton, and the pounding in my head would not cease.

The conversational chit-chat of voices I didn't recognize and smoke caused me to breathe in an irregular pattern. My legs throbbed and my neck ached. In fact, if there was a part of my body not in pain, at the moment, I was unaware of it.

"Sheretta, can you tell me your last name?" asked the blonde firefighter who appeared to be fresh out of high school. "What day of September is it?" she questioned.

Unable to speak, I squeezed my eyes while making an attempt to block out everything going on around me, with hopes the pain would cease and this was just another nightmare. I knew it was the last day of September, but I couldn't utter a word.

As they slid me inside the new state-of-the-art rescue transport vehicle, I heard the driver as he communicated via two-way radio. I looked around and saw lights lining the walls, metal cabinets, and other medical supplies.

"I have a thirty-eight-year-old female with lacerations to the face and arms." He paused as he examined my leg. "There is severe-bruising on the right leg."

Feeling spots of warm patches on my face and arms alarmed me. In an attempt to raise my arms, it was then I realized I couldn't move.

I must have fainted, because when I came to, I was no longer in the rescue transport vehicle. The pounding rain and blackened sky were now visible. I was under the covered emergency entrance leading into Turner Memorial Hospital, a familiar place to me. I reflected on the days I'd spent there when Monroe had been shot in the line of duty during an attempted bank robbery at the Bank of Turner.

Immobile, I laid on the stretcher looking for recognizable faces. I was able to visualize men and women in white lab coats and nurses in blue scrubs on both sides of the stretcher. The blinding fluorescent lighting at the emergency exit was brighter than I'd noticed before. The smell of alcohol and disinfectant stung my nose. They rolled me through the halls at what seemed to be racecar speed and placed me in a rectangular room. The room contained tubing in assorted sizes, gauze, other medical supplies, and a red sharps container. The putty-colored walls seemed to be twirling.

A man's scream captured my attention. "Help me!" His voice was weak, his scream pitiful.

I cried as they transferred me to the bed. Still on the plastic backboard, I felt helpless. The doctors and nurses spoke medical jargon. Beside the fact I was frightened and disoriented, exhaustion consumed me. The skin on my arms and face felt tight. I rolled my eyes downward as I glimpsed dried blood on my cheeks. To no avail, I made another attempt to touch my face.

I murmured, "I can't move my arms."

"Lay still, Ms. Miller. Your arms are still strapped to the bed rails. We want to make
sure you don't have any broken bones. You're scheduled for x-rays," said a female physician that stood at my bedside, flipping through what appeared to be my chart.

"Hmmm, I want Monroe," I whispered.

The nurse that accompanied the physician replied, "Please be still. I know you're uncomfortable, but we don't know how badly you're injured. You've got to stay still. Your family has been notified. I'm sure they'll be here soon."

"Where is she? Where is she?" yelled a deep voice in the hallway.

It was then I recognized that the baritone voice belonged to Monroe.

He rushed into the room and stood just close enough to be in my view. A look of relief covered his face as soon as he made eye contact with me.

"Are you okay? What happened?" he rattled on. "It's my fault. I should've been there on time." He sobbed as he dropped his head in his palms.

"Officer, she'll be just fine. Please calm down," said the nurse, while recording my vitals. "We're taking her to get x-rays shortly. She should be back in a few minutes."

"Can I go with her?"

"No, she'll be fine, but you're more than welcome to wait here until she returns," she growled.

I looked in his face as he stood by my side. Again, I saw the look in his eyes I'd seen before. I was almost in a state of shock, but I remembered that look. I heard the rain hitting the roof of the older building, while the lightening glistened past the oblong window.

"Sheretta, baby, I'm here. I love you."

Looking at him, I felt safe, but couldn't utter a word.

Rubbing my arm, Monroe said, "You'll be fine."

The male x-ray tech stepped in and announced, "Officer, she'll be back from x-ray in no time at all."

"Can I go with her?" he asked again.

"No, sir. She'll be fine. I promise," the x-ray tech replied.

Monroe bent down, kissed me on the cheek, and said, "I love you."

As they rolled me out of the room, I heard the portable radio Monroe often wore when he was off duty. "Attention, I need the attention of all Turner police and rescue staff. We are preparing for a possible hurricane. Thus far, we have had over four inches of rain and high wind gusts. Please contact your shift leader as soon as possible."

He looked into my eyes as they rounded the corner with me on the portable bed.

After hearing the announcement, I knew he'd be gone upon my return.

*****

I lay in the room and waited for what seemed like hours. I then remembered just why I was in Turner Memorial in the first place. The strange black car that was following me caused me to run off the road and plunge down the embankment into the ravine. All I could think of was the fact I almost lost my life.

Exhaustion must have crept in, because when I woke up, I was on the bed traveling through the halls of Turner Memorial. I looked up into the eyes of an elderly male attendant. Before I knew anything, I was back in the rectangular room. I saw Monroe's back as he faced the window. He turned as soon as he heard the squeaky wheels of the bed.

"Here she is," said the elderly attendant.

"Thanks for taking good care of her," Monroe told him as he walked to my side and assisted the technician with maneuvering the bed.

"You're welcome, officer. We're in the middle of shift changes, so it took a little longer than expected." The elderly gentleman locked the wheels while he waited for a nursing assistant to help him transfer me back to my bed.

"That's okay. Thanks again."

Monroe pulled a tissue from the tissue box and wiped my tears just before he whispered in my ear.

"Sheretta, I love you. I'm so sorry this happened." He paused. "What happened? You're always such a careful driver." He rubbed my hand and placed a kiss on my lips.

A combination of rain, meds, and exhaustion were about to win the battle. My eyes were heavy. The smell of the disinfectant was pungent, while the sound coming from the overhead paging system confirmed this was no dream; I was in the hospital.

The dawning of a new day was my alarm clock. Visits from nurses through the night hindered my sleep. The overcast day was dim, but I was glad to be alive to see it, even if I was seeing it from a hospital bed. My eyes were heavy even after a night of rest. I cast my eyes to the recliner in front of the window that Monroe occupied. He'd always been a sound sleeper, and last night was no different.

I admired him as he slept. His flawless skin seemed a bit rugged. The beard that was peeking through hid hints of silver strands. He began to shift in the recliner. His eyes popped open and affixed on me. Before I could say anything, he was at my bedside.

"Good morning," he uttered.

"Morning," I managed after licking my lips, taking a deep breath, and shifting myself into the center of the bed.

"Let me help you," he pleaded.

"I'm good. Did you stay here all night?"

"Yes," he responded, rubbing his eyes.

"You didn't have to do that."

"I needed to make sure you were okay. Your dad called last night after you dozed off."

"What did he want?"

"His plane should be landing in a couple of hours."

I sucked my teeth as I rolled my eyes up toward the ceiling. "Why?"

"He was concerned. I told him that you were okay, but he insisted on coming."

I shivered as the pain in my right leg shot upward, causing me to squint and grip the bed sheet. The monitor began

beeping, and a nurse was in the room before either of us could press
the help button.

"Ms. Miller, I need you to relax and lie still. Your blood pressure is a bit high. I see it's time for your meds. I'll be back shortly."

I looked at Monroe and cried.

"Calm down, baby. I promise I'll be here with you."

"Why did you call him of all people?" I whimpered, raised my head, and threw my covers back with my left arm, only to feel intense pain in my arm and side. "Oh Lord!" I screeched as my head fell back on the pillow.

The nurse reset the monitors, fluffed my pillows, wiped my mouth with a moist cloth, and gave me a sip of ginger ale before exiting my room.

"What did you have to tell the Honorable Judge Robert Miller to get him to leave his trophy wife, uppity kids, and his home on the hill?"

"You're going to upset yourself. All I told him was that you'd been in an accident. Before I could tell him that you'd be okay, he told me that he'd be here in the morning."

"I just want to be left alone. He has a way of making me feel less than human." I raised my hands to cover my face.

"Sheretta, let it go," Monroe uttered as he looked at me.

Silence plagued the room until the door opened.

"Ms. Miller, I'm back with something for you." The nurse looked at my admission's bracelet and matched the information on the chart before giving my meds to me.

I had some broken ribs, and with even the slightest movement, I felt pure pain. The sound of the overhead paging system startled me.

The nurse placed a white pill cup in my one hand and a cup of water in the other. "Relax, Ms. Miller. This will ease your pain."

Monroe made his way back to the recliner, leaned forward, and dropped his head. It was there he remained until the nurse left the room.

"Monroe, please come here." I extended my hand in his direction.

With a flick of his wrist, he glanced at his watch, walked over to the bed, and took my hand. "It's almost seven in the morning. Your father's plane will land in about an hour. I told him that I'd pick him up," he said firmly. "I'm going to take a shower, change clothes, call Grandma Tate, and then notify Captain Pierce that I'll be out for a few days."

"Well, I can tell you one thing. If Daddy shows up with that high and mighty attitude of his, he'll not be welcome here," I snapped.

"Sheretta, let it go. You need to rest, allow your body time to heal, and not hold on to the past. You're a wonderful woman, and I just don't know why you can't get past this ordeal with your father. What in the world is going on with you two?"

"Just leave, Monroe!" I yelled.

As he turned to leave, he shook his head. He walked out the door, never looking back.

As I lay in the bed, the monitor began to beep. My breathing became erratic. Nurses and nursing assistants appeared out of nowhere. Loud beeping and conversations going on around me frightened me all the more.

When I woke, I discovered I was in a different room. All I could see were bright lights and tubes. My arms were weighed down with tubes, and my head throbbed. The pain in my right leg seemed to have intensified. I closed my eyes and inhaled, only to realize I was in the Intensive Care Unit. I knew because Grandma Tate spent six weeks in the I.C.U. after her heart attack three years ago. When I attempted to shift positions, I heard voices.

"Sheretta, baby, it's Daddy. I'm here."

My eyes popped open. The voice was none other than that of my dear father. I'd hoped it was all a bad dream: the accident, my hospital stay, and the vision of my dad standing only feet away.

Remembering my manners, I said, "Hello, Dad."

I'd almost forgotten how handsome he was. His honey complexion paired with his salt and pepper hair made him look as distinguished and important as he'd always thought he was.

"Hi, Princess. How are you? Daddy's here. You don't have to worry anymore," he said, bending down to kiss my cheek.

"I'll be fine in a few days. I don't know why Monroe made such a big deal out of a little fender bender," I said, then peered at Monroe.

"Princess, I saw your vehicle. My dear, it was definitely more than a fender bender." My father looked from me to the monitor connected to my stiff body.

Through weak eyes, I gazed at Monroe with a look he'd not seen since I'd changed my ways. In a split second, he turned and looked away.

"Sheretta, what happened?"

"It all happened so fast, Daddy." I paused. "I remember sitting on the bench reading while I waited for Monroe. The next thing I knew, a black car raced into the WeCumm parking lot and was heading in my direction. I didn't know what to do."

I stopped speaking as my mind drifted back to that dreadful experience.

"Why didn't you tell me this last night?" Monroe snapped.

"Hold on one minute, Monroe. Sheretta has had a near death experience. Don't you dare raise your voice at her." He looked at Monroe and walked in his direction.

"I'm not yelling. It's as if I'm always the last person to know what's going on," he said as he rose from the chair.

They stood inches apart staring each other down. Monroe's nostrils flared while Dad's jaw stiffened as I watched. They turned in my direction and made their way to me in unison.

"I'm sorry, Princess. We're both concerned about you, that's all."

"Sheretta, you know I love you. I've told you not to keep anything from me..."

Daddy interrupted him. "Princess, finish telling me what happened."

"A black car was chasing me."

"What did the driver look like?" Daddy asked.

"I couldn't see anything. The windows were tinted. I didn't know what to do, so I jumped inside the truck and drove as fast as I could. The last thing I remember was reaching into my handbag to get my cell phone so I could call you." I looked at Monroe.

Monroe moved my hair from my eyes and bent to place a kiss on my lips.

The door swung open and a new nurse appeared. She had to have been in her late fifties. Her full figure was neat; she smelled light and flowery; and her pearl necklace accented her pearl earrings. Her beautiful smile and flawless skin captured the attention of men.

"Hello, I'm Nurse McQueen. I'll be Sheretta's nurse for the day," she said, smiling at my dad as if he were the patient. "I'm sorry, there are limited visiting hours in this unit. I'm going to have to ask you to leave," she continued as she looked at Dad again.

"Let me introduce myself. I'm Judge Robert Miller, Sheretta's father. I flew in from New York to check on my princess. I'm sure you can find it in your heart to let us stay a little longer." He flashed his million-dollar smile, which included perfect pearly whites and a gold tooth.

"I guess a few minutes won't hurt," replied Nurse McQueen as she blushed before exiting the room.

While watching him turn on his charm, I immediately remembered part of the reason I dreaded his presence. His smug look, expensive clothing, jewelry, and way with women almost always seemed to capture the attention of the female specimen of all ages.

His cell began to vibrate. He retreated to the corner to take the call. I know he knew that cell phones weren't allowed in this section of the hospital, but like always, he breaks the rules when it suits his purpose.

He stood near the window whispering on his cell phone. His back was facing us, and I could still smell the expensive cologne. His gold bracelet glistened in the morning sunlight.

"Once again, the storm has passed us by. I'm going back to the scene of the accident. I want to see if I can find any clues. I'll call Captain Pierce and have him meet me. Is there anything you can remember about the black car? Did it have any fancy rims or South Carolina plates?" Monroe asked, almost in a whisper.

"It happened so fast. It was dusk dark. I did notice the headlights were those new blue lights. The windows were dark, so I couldn't see the driver's face." I whimpered and closed my eyes to hold back the tears.

"Hush, baby. Get some rest. I'll be back," he whispered.

When I saw Daddy turning in our direction, I could tell he was ending the call. His tailored dress slack, Italian leather shoes, starched lavender shirt, and silk tie were obviously expensive. He was a powerful man and he knew it.

"I'm sorry; I had to take that call," he offered.

"I've got some work to do. I should see you in a few hours," said Monroe as he rubbed the area of my hand not occupied by tubes.

"Princess, I'll be back before you know it. I'm going to get a rental car and visit some family in the area. Have you talked with your aunt or uncles lately?"

"No, she's always so busy. I did see her in the grocery store the day before the storm. She seemed a bit preoccupied, but you know she's never had much to do with me. Uncle Martin and Uncle Billy are always gone to visit their children or on some extravagant vacation with one of their latest women."

"You know my sister is a different type of woman. She loves you, Princess." He paused. "She is a bit strange, always has been. As a little girl, she played by herself. Let's just say she's one of a kind. But, she sure can cook." He laughed. "You're right, though. Those brothers of mine can't stay still for long."

Monroe made his way to the door. It was as if he was trying his level best to leave Dad behind.

"Umm....Monroe, will you drop me off at the rental agency. I have some people I'd like to visit while I'm home, and I don't want to be a hindrance to you," he said, hurrying across the room.

"How long are you planning to stay?"

"I'm not sure, Princess. I've got my bench covered indefinitely. I'm going to make sure you're okay. Now that it looks like someone deliberately ran you off the road, I'm going to make sure whoever's responsible is punished. You know I've still got contacts here," he boasted, while sticking out his chest. "Princess, don't you worry about a thing. The guilty party will pay dearly." He bent down and kissed my forehead. "I'll wait outside, Monroe."

"I'll be right out."

"Monroe, please be nice," I pleaded once Daddy was on the other side of the door.

"Okay. If you promise to get some rest, I'll tolerate him. He won't be here forever."

"Monroe, I just remembered Deacon McCall was at the accident. I heard him call my name. He must have told the paramedics who I was, because they called me by name," I managed to say as I shifted positions. "I've got to call and thank him."

"He called the station and left a message for me. That's how I found out you'd been in an accident. I'll go to WeCumm later today and thank him. Maybe he saw something or someone that will help us solve this mystery."

"Baby, please tell him thanks for me."

Monroe frowned. "Who was at WeCumm when you left?"

"The parking lot was empty. I was the last employee to leave that day. Why do you ask?"

"Just wondering. I'll see you in a bit."

"I love you. I'm so sleepy." I yawned as he left.

Ten Minutes Later in Monroe's Car

"Monroe, I know we don't always see eye to eye, but we do have one thing in common. We both love Sheretta. I will not rest until I get to the bottom of this. Princess is a darn good driver; you and I both know it. This was no accident."

"Something sounds fishy. After I drop you off, I'm going to meet Captain Pierce at the scene. The rain will have tampered with some of the evidence, but I believe we'll be able to find something that will tell us who's behind this," Monroe said, biting the inside of his jaw.

"I'll call you as soon as I've visited my sister and brothers. I left messages telling them that I'd be here today. I know my sister has cooked a feast," Robert boasted. "Is Tucker still the chief?"

"Yes. There's been some talk about him retiring, but you know folks in Turner. They're always gossiping about something or someone," Monroe chuckled.

"We attended school together. I'll pay him a visit tomorrow."

"Since he lost his wife to breast cancer, he's been depressed. I'm sure he'd be glad to see you." Monroe turned into the rental agency and put the car in gear. "Do you need me to come in and make sure you get what you need?" he asked, then honked the horn and waved at one of the former members of Mount Pisgah who left and went over to Deliverance Temple.

"No, I'll be fine. When my wife called to check on Sheretta this morning, she told me that she made a reservation for me. You know she wanted to come, but Princess doesn't care for her," he offered as he reached for the handle, opened the door, and stepped out. "Thanks, Monroe."

After taking time to jot down some notes, Monroe looked in the rearview mirror as he put the car in reverse and breathed a sigh of relief. Less than five minutes later, his cell phone rang.

"Hello." He paused as he waited for the caller to speak. "This is Officer Monroe Tate."

"This is Beverly from Turner Rentals. I need a reference on Mr. Robert Miller. Could you verify that he's an acquaintance of yours? He listed you as a personal reference."

"Yes, he's a friend of mine and a schoolmate of the chief of police, as well. He's a judge in New York City. He's the founding partner of Miller & Sons Attorneys at Law. If I need to rent the car in my name, I have no problem with that.

Let me give you a word of advice. Just rent the car to him. I'll come in and sign for it later, if need be."

"That won't be necessary. Thank you very much, Officer Tate. That's all I need. Have a nice day," she replied with an aggravated tone.

Monroe chucked. "You, too," he said before the agent disconnected the call, then thought to himself, *You needed me after all, huh?*

*****

At the scene of the accident, they combed the area what seemed like a hundred times. At the point of impact, they retrieved some of Sheretta's personal items, vehicle parts, and even a twenty-dollar bill. The swampy area was muddy and stagnant. It was as if they moved every blade of grass and every pebble on the ground.

Looking down just off the roadway, Captain Pierce said, "Tate, do you see what I see? I've been on the force more than twenty years, and I've never seen tire tracks of this kind in Turner. These tracks are from specialty tires usually used on souped-up cars. I'll make an impression and send it to the lab in Charleston. The technician there owes me a favor."

The portly, cocoa complexion man had worked his way up police ranks after eight years in the Marines. He was often silent, but when he spoke, you could trust his opinion. Still being single after a nasty divorce, he often spent his weekends working extra duty and fishing.

"Thanks for your help. I'm clueless in this case."

"Tate, that's understandable. You're too close to see the obvious to make an airtight case against the culprit or culprits. I don't have much to do these days, now I do?" he said as he walked back to an unmarked patrol car. "Trust me, I know how you feel about Sheretta. When you love someone, it's difficult to mask."

"You're right. Thanks again," replied Monroe, while he stood looking at the area that almost claimed the life of the woman he loved, the woman he intended to marry.

*****

Back at the Hospital

"Sheretta, I'm so sorry to hear about your accident. WeCumm is buzzing about your mishap." Samantha stood by the bed wearing a navy business suit, a pair of four-inch pumps, and two layers of makeup.

"Thanks for the flowers and card. I love roses. Please be sure to thank everyone in the office for me. By the way, you look terrific," I remarked. "Ms. Hardy came by earlier to check on me. I was glad to see her."

"Oh, she did?" Samantha asked. "I didn't know Ms. Hardy was coming by. She's always so prim and proper. Anyway, is there anything I can do for you?" Samantha asked, while easing over to the table where the flowers sat. "I love these orchids and lilies. They're gorgeous."

"They're from my daddy."

"Oh, how lovely. When's he coming?" she inquired.

"He's already here. He flew in this morning." I shifted in bed.

"You're lucky; you have two men who absolutely adore you. Well, I've got to be going. I'm sure you'll be back at work in no time at all, but take your time. You need your rest. We'll take care of everything at WeCumm during your absence," Samantha proclaimed as she picked up her leather handbag and reached for the door handle just before she paused. "I'm really glad you're okay. Remember, I'm just a phone call away."

Samantha's full figure and stylish hair often caused men to take a second look. Her hair was always immaculate, and the dimple in her right cheek was noticeable. In her earlier years, she modeled for agencies in Charleston and Myrtle Beach.

71

Sleep was my BFF. I slept more in the last twenty-four hours than I had in the last twenty-four months. Two things I despised while hospitalized were the nurses coming in and out every hour on the hour and the overhead paging system that always seemed to wake me as soon as I dozed off. Nurse McQueen came in my room so often that I thought I was the only patient in the unit...heck, the entire floor. I'm sure I had received more leg rubs, monitor checks, and pillow fluffs than all the other patients combined.

"Ms. Miller, can I get you anything?" she asked. "If you need anything, just press the call button and I'll be right here," she offered as she bent to pick up a piece of paper from the floor. "The doctor said you were healing nicely."

"Thank you," I said before yawning and drifting off again.

*****

After knocking on the door of the newly remodeled country house, the five-foot, eleven-inch man turned to look over the land he once played on. With his hands stuffed in his pockets, he strolled to the edge of the porch and admired the place he called home for over twenty years of his life. No matter what was going on, the lake on the farm always seemed to provide peace and tranquility. He smiled and shook his head as he cast his eyes on the weeping willow east of the property. It apparently brought back memories of the days when they would gather on the grounds for family reunions, home goings, and birthday celebrations. The old barn in the rear also held memories. Memories of the day his great-grandmother Miller had a heart attack in that same barn would always surface when he stepped foot on this land.

The squeaky screen door swung open. "Bobby, I'm glad to see you," cried Lucy as she hugged her big-shot brother. "Boy, come on in here."

She backed up so he could enter the foyer, which led to the immaculate living room.

"Sis, I'm glad to see you, too." He gave her a big bear hug. "I was coming home next month for the family reunion, but my princess needs me now. Did you get my message letting you know I was in town?"

"No. I'm terrible about checking my messages. I was going to call you. I had no idea you'd be here so soon. When I heard about the wreck, I knew you were coming, though. I just didn't know when." She paused before continuing. "Lord have mercy. I saw it in the paper this morning, and it was even on television last night. I saw Sheretta a few weeks ago. Is she alright?" she asked, but didn't wait for a response. "I called your house this morning, and that wife of yours said she'd tell you I called. Not at any time before I hung up did she tell me that you were here. That's why I ain't got nothing to do with her."

"Sheretta's broken up a bit. She's young, strong, and healthy. She'll be up and about in no time," he stated, finally finding an opportunity to get a word in. "How are you, sis?" he then asked as he looked in her eyes, avoiding the wife comment.

"I'm okay," she responded before turning and walking into the kitchen.

"Sis, really, how are you?" He trailed behind her. "I mean, really."

"Bobby, time has healed some wounds. I'm good. Come on in here and eat. I've cooked baked chicken, corn, string beans, and potato salad for dinner."

"That sounds good to me."

She still had the figure of a twenty-year-old and wavy hair that flowed down past her shoulders. Her perfect brown complexion was aging. Her high cheekbones had a natural hint of red. The Native American heritage was obvious in Lucy

Miller's appearance. Her heart was never the same after the loss of their great grandmother, who was the matriarch of the Miller family. She'd spent more time with Great-grandmother Miller than she did with her mother.

"Lucy, the food was delicious, as usual. I'm going back to the hospital to see Sheretta, but I should be back around nine. Is my room ready?" Robert asked.

"Bobby, you know I keep my house ready. One can never tell when one of the Miller boys will return." She laughed.

"Thanks, Lucy," he said, then walked out the side door.

*****

"Princess, I'm back. I've been calling every now and then to check on you. Nurse McQueen said you were resting comfortably." Robert paused and looked over at the table where the flowers sat. "I see my flowers arrived."

He walked over to the huge arrangement of orchids, lilies, baby's breath, and assorted greenery and took a whiff.

"Who sent the roses?" he asked after turning his nose up and walking back to the bed.

His starched jeans, orange Miller & Sons polo, and casual shoes screamed money.

"The roses are from the WeCumm team. Samantha brought them by," I said. "They're so thoughtful. Things have been happening so fast that I didn't get a chance to call and tell you the good news."

"Let me guess. You're going back to school to complete your law degree," my dad said, beaming with joy. "You know you can always come to work at Miller & Sons." He chuckled. "Well, of course, we'd change the name to Miller Family Attorneys at Law. Since I've left the practice, your brothers need someone to watch over them," he teased.

A deep breath later, I said, "No, Daddy. I'm the new accounting supervisor at WeCumm. I replaced Kyle Carroll after he was terminated."

"Oh? When did all this happen?" he forced.

Just then, there was a knock at the door.

"Come in," he said, then turned to me. "We'll finish this conversation later."

"Ms. Miller, I'll be leaving in a bit. Wanted to make sure you were all set for the night," Nurse McQueen said, twisting her way to the monitor. She picked up my chart and looked at my identification band like she hadn't been doing it all day. "How are you feeling, my dear?" she asked as she patted my shoulder.

"I'm sore here." I touched an area of my chest.

"Let me get you something for pain. Your doctor prescribed something; it'll make you drowsy, though."

She walked toward the door, almost stumbling on the IV pole. Jumping to her rescue, Dad caught her in his arms.

"Thank you, Mr. Miller," she said, while smoothing her uniform down with her hands as she exited the room.

"You're welcome, Nurse McQueen."

A couple minutes later, she returned.

"I'm back." She placed a pill in my left hand and a cup of water in my right. "If you continue to improve, you'll be released in a few days. The doctor will speak with you about arranging physical therapy after your release."

"Thank you," I responded after swallowing the pill and water.

"You're quite welcome. I'll see you tomorrow. If you need anything, remember to hit the call button."

It was as if I'd taken a sleeping pill. Everything got fuzzy, but I do know Dad left the room on the trail of the nurse of the day. Although I was in a groggy state, I could hear them conversing right outside my room.

75

"Nurse McQueen, I'd like to thank you personally for taking care of my princess."

"You're quite welcome. That's why I'm here."

"I'd like to show you my appreciation. Would you like to join me for a cup of coffee?" he asked her.

"Sure. I'll be ready in a second. I think it'd be better if I meet you offsite."

"Turner's Cafe in an hour?" he suggested.

"Terrific."

"Princess, I'm a bit tired," he told me upon re-entering my room. "I've had a long day. Lucy will be waiting up for me, and I don't want to cause her to worry. You know how she gets. Plus, it's important that you get plenty of rest," he offered and then kissed my forehead.

"Goodnight, Dad. I'll see you in the morning."

"Love you, Princess."

"Love you, too."

I watched television as I pondered what lie ahead. My recovery would take a while, and with the new position, I wondered if I'd be able to maintain the pace.

"Lord, please tell me what to do. I need you now," I prayed.

Then, out of nowhere, I heard a soft voice reply, "Trust me."

A tap on the door ended my praise session.

"Come in," I called out.

"Hi, beautiful. How are you this evening?" asked Monroe. He smiled at me holding his blue Bible case.

"I'm tired, but I feel better now. I'm a party pooper. Nurse McQueen gave me a pain pill, and it's kicking in now."

"Well, I'm going to let you get some rest. I'll be right over there." He pointed to the chair in the corner. "I went by the house to pick up my Bible. I'm behind in my reading. So, while you're sleeping, I'll be able to get caught up."

"I am, too. I haven't read my daily devotional in days," I said, licking my lips.

"You thirsty?" he asked.

"Can I get a sip of ginger ale?" I managed.

"Sure. What did you have to eat today?"

"Beef with broth, mixed veggies, a roll, and Jello. My taste buds are gone. Everything tastes like medicine."

"As soon as you're up and about, dinner's my treat, baby," he said, while helping me to a sitting position and holding the straw for me.

"Thanks, Monroe. Good night," I said, offering a smile as I laid back and got comfortable.

"You're welcome."

*****

The morning was overcast and the smell of rain was refreshing. The view of Monroe sleeping in the same room gave me a sense of security. I had a flashback of the dark car closing in on me as I tried to get to safety. When I closed my eyes, I saw brush, breaking glass, a view of my spinning car, the airbag exploding in my face, and heard the sound of a loud thump.

The next sound was that of the overhead paging system.

"Code blue 223 north; code blue 223 north."

Monroe jumped up from a deep sleep and rushed over to my bed.

"Sheretta, are you okay? I heard code blue," he said, his eyes expanding with fear.

"Monroe, my room number is 222 north," I told him as we listened to the commotion outside my door.

It was as if a herd of elephants were charging past. The older facility was definitely not soundproof. We heard almost every sound coming from the room next door.

77

Monroe rested his hand on mine and began to pray. "Father God, we come to you as humble as we know how. You're the most high God and we honor your name. Please offer strength and wisdom to the patient now in distress as well as their family. We know you can do all things. We're asking for a healing, dear Lord. In your name, we pray. Amen."

"I thank God for a praying man. His will shall be done," I reaffirmed as I opened my hand.

Monroe took my hand, kissed the back of it, and returned to the corner to rest.

Hours later, an older brunette with a missing front tooth came to clean the room. "Good morning. How are you today? I'll be just a minute."

In her gloved hand, she held a roll of trash bags. As she scurried about cleaning the room, she sang softly. I noticed how beautiful her voice was; it was calming.

"You sing beautifully," Monroe told her.

She blushed. " Thank you for the compliment. Young man, back in the day, I could really sing." She laughed. "Life has its way of maturing your talents. Well, I'm all done. I hope things work well for you, ma'am." She then bid us farewell with a smile.

Nurses, nurses, and more nurses came. One to check this and one to check that. It was non-stop for a while. The young assistant who came to bathe me was nice, but it was obvious she was preoccupied. She said less than twenty words the entire time she was in my room.

A knock at the door alerted us to a visitor.

"Come in," Monroe said as he made his way to the door to greet the guest.

"Good morning, Sister Miller, Brother Tate," said Pastor Walters. He shook Monroe's hand, then walked over to the bed and looked at me with a soothing smile. "My child, how are you this morning? I wanted to give you some time to heal before rushing over."

"Thanks for coming, Pastor. I'm feeling better and ready to go home."

"Sister, have you ever thought this could be the Father's way of telling you that He needs more of your time?"

Monroe stood to the side in silence as Pastor Walters spoke.

"Perhaps you're right, Pastor. I saw my life flash before my eyes. I prayed and cried as I went down the steep embankment. I was terrified."

The beeping monitor claimed our attention. As it became louder, the numbers and patterns went crazy. A nurse appeared in seconds.

"Hello, I'm your nurse for the day," she said, while resetting the monitor before checking my pulse and heart rate. She then examined the monitor and cords closely.

Her face was familiar, but I didn't know her name.

"Ms. Miller, I'm going to ask you to lie still for a bit. How are you feeling?" she inquired.

"Is everything alright?" Monroe asked.

"She's okay. Her blood pressure is a tad bit high, but her meds will bring it down. Have you been resting at night?"

"I feel fine. I'm a little sleepy, and my chest hurts," I responded. "I doze for a while. Then I wake up and stare at the ceiling."

"I'm going to check and see if the doctor has ordered anything for your pain. If so, I'll be back. I'll also ask about something to help you sleep. Reverend Walters, it's so good to see you."

"Bless you, my sister. How have you been?" he asked with what appeared to be genuine concern as he walked in her direction.

"I'm doing well." She hesitated for a moment before asking, "Would you mind stopping at the nurse's station before you leave?"

"I sure will," he answered with that humble smile he always wore.

As Monroe and Pastor conversed, I fell asleep. Every now and then, I'd wake up and look in their direction, only to see them laughing and talking.

"Monroe, Sheretta is fast asleep, so I'm going to ease out. Please tell her that I'll be praying for her. I'll be back tomorrow." He stopped just feet from the door. "By the way, did you know that Mother Gray had a heart attack and was admitted yesterday?"

"No. How is she?" he asked with concern. "I've been so preoccupied with everything going on with Sheretta that I must admit I've been out of the loop. Chances are Grandma Tate knows and hasn't said anything. My prayers are with her and her family," Monroe said as they walked to the door.

After Pastor Walters left, Monroe returned to his seat in the corner, read his devotional, and dozed off.

*****

At The Offices of WeCumm

"Hello, Samantha Sharpe speaking. How may I help you?"

"Samantha, Ms. Hardy would like to see you in her office," said Ms. Hardy's receptionist.

"I can be there in about five minutes. Is that okay?" Samantha asked.

"Yes, that'll be fine."

I wonder what this is about, Samantha thought as she hung up the phone. *I've done my job. It's always something.*

She grabbed a pen and pad and stood to leave. Before leaving, she took a mirror from her purse to make sure her hair was in place and to touch up her lipstick.

The perking coffee and the aromas of the heated staff meals coming from the lounge reminded Samantha that she hadn't eaten lunch. Deacon McCall was scrubbing the floor when she rounded the corner to the Human Resources wing. Three yellow wet floor signs trailed the center of the hall.

"Hello, Deacon McCall," she said as she took careful steps past him.

"Hi, Samantha," he replied, pushing the mop back and forth.

As she approached the circular reception station, she noticed it was unoccupied. Before she reached the station, the elderly receptionist appeared with a coffee mug in her hand.

"Hello, you must be Samantha," she greeted with a smile. "Ms. Hardy is expecting you. You may go in." She pointed to the door clearly labeled with Ms. Hardy's name and title.

"Thanks," Samantha said, then walked in the direction she'd been directed.

The spacious office contained an oak bookcase with no less than fifty books. There were no photographs, while six paintings lined the walls. The stern look on Ms. Hardy's face was peculiar.

"Good evening, Ms. Sharpe. Thank you for taking time out of your busy schedule to see me. With Sheretta Miller being out, I know your department is shorthanded. I understand she'll be out for at least thirty days, so I'm in need of someone to fill her position until she returns."

A look of confusion covered Samantha's face as she sat in the leather chair trying to contain her emotions, anger, confusion, and then happiness.

"I've been here eight years, so I believe I can handle the position. But, I have one question. If Sheretta doesn't return, will I be able to remain in the position permanently?" Samantha asked.

Ms. Hardy looked at Samantha with a bewildered expression. "As I said earlier, she'll be back in about thirty days. As other positions become vacant, you are more than welcome to apply," she finally responded as she fingered her burgundy pen.

"Thank you for the opportunity. I'm sure I'll be able to handle the job," said Samantha. "Is there anything else?"

"Can you move into her office tomorrow? There are records and files that I want to remain in her office under lock and key." She paused as she awaited an answer.

"Yes, I can move in tomorrow. You won't be disappointed," Samantha told her, then got up to leave.

Ms. Hardy's eyebrows were now bunched in the middle.

"You're welcome. I'll alert the staff that you'll be the interim Accounting Supervisor. "

"Thanks again," Samantha said as she walked out of the office.

All Samantha could do when she returned to her desk was smile and daydream.

"I'm going to pay Sheretta another visit," she said while staring into space and licking her lips. "First thing I'm going to do is go shopping. My first day in my new position calls for a new suit."

The remainder of the day breezed by, and all Samantha did was think about her new job.

"Ugh! I hate pumping gas," she growled as she pulled into the convenience store's parking lot. "Why is it when I need gas everyone else does, too?"

Stepping from the car was a chore, but her tired legs made the journey. There were no less than ten people in line ahead of her and only one register open.

The attendant on duty rolled her eyes upward in her head as the elderly man held up the line buying lottery tickets.

"I want a number six, two number thirteens, and four of them number seven, one-dollar scratch offs," he mumbled.

Holding the twenty-dollar bill in her hand, Samantha's focus remained on the movement of the line, or the fact that the line was barely moving.

She shuffled from one foot to the other in order to ease the pain in her feet. Her heels had done a number on her feet. She'd walked back and forth visualizing in her mind how she planned to redo Sheretta's office and mold it to suit her taste. Finally, it was her turn. She handed the clerk the money.

"Twenty on pump three, please," she said and then turned to walk out the door.

Thump!

"I'm sorry," said the handsome, well-dressed gentleman.

Samantha bent her neck back to see who was going to get told off.

"I'm sorry, miss. I didn't see you. Are you okay?" he asked, while holding on to her waist with arms of steel.

Samantha was rendered immobile. All she could do was stare into the marble-like eyes of the man who smelled like heaven on earth. His chest was broad, and his smile was as big as a half moon, displaying pearly whites. While she anticipated what his next words would be, she fell into a trance.

A fine brother like this in Turner? I've got to be dreaming. He smells good and looks good. His teeth are pearly white; he has a pleasant disposition; and to top it off, he's a gentleman, she thought.

"Oh, I'm fine. I'm okay. It was an accident," she said, flashing her dimpled smile and remaining in his arms as if she never wanted this moment to end.

"Let me make it up to you. I couldn't help but overhear your conversation with the clerk as you paid for the gas. I'd be more than happy to pump it for you."

"Thank you."

He extended his hand to initiate a handshake. "Let's try this again. Hello, my name is Daryl Chase. It's nice to meet you."

Samantha extended her hand to take his. "Hello, nice to meet you, as well. I'm Samantha Sharpe." She admired the softness of his hand and the sparkle in his eyes.

As they walked out, he held the door while she exited. Samantha walked as she did when she was a model twenty years ago. It was as if her feet had been massaged and suddenly healed.

As he pumped the gas, they stood and talked like they'd known each other for years. When they did look up again, the pump was at thirty-eight dollars and climbing.

"Wow. I've gone over. I'll go ahead and fill up the tank," Daryl said as he reached for his wallet. "Here's my number. Please give me a call." He removed a card and placed it in her hand. "I'll take care of the gas. It's my fault," he said before walking toward the store.

Samantha stared out the window without so much as a blink of her eye. Her trance-like state was out of character for her. Her strong personality was often criticized.

"My next stop will be Turner Memorial," she said as she looked at her gas gauge. "Thank you, Lord. And to think I didn't want to stop and get gas." She laughed before pulling off.

*****

Samantha pulled into the parking lot of Turner Memorial Hospital and proceeded to drive until she found a parking space close to the door. She looked in the mirror, making sure she still looked her best.

"Sheretta will be surprised to see me. I just need to make sure she stays in the hospital a little longer," she said to herself before opening the door.

Before heading to Sheretta's room, Samantha stopped in the gift ship to pick up a book for her.

"Hello, how are you?" Samantha asked the lady behind the counter.

"I'm well and how about you?" the young lady responded.

"I'm great," Samantha replied.

As Samantha made her way to Sheretta's room, she thought about her gas station encounter and smiled. She saw nurses and doctors in a huddle at the nurse's station and walked by as if she were an immediate family member. Samantha knew the Turner Memorial staff were sticklers about abiding by the designated visiting hours. When she entered the open door, the silhouette of a tall man facing the window caught her attention.

"Hello," she whispered after realizing Sheretta was asleep.

"Hello," said the man as he turned with a cell phone in hand. "I'll call you back. Sheretta has company." He ended the call and stuffed the phone in its holster while staring at Samantha. "Can I help you?" he asked, his lips forming a frown.

"I'm Samantha Sharpe. I work at WeCumm with Sheretta." She reached out to shake his hand.

"I'm Robert Miller, Sheretta's father. Who did you say you were?" he asked as if he was questioning a witness on the stand.

After a few seconds, he decided it would be rude if he didn't greet his daughter's guest with decency. Still staring, he cleared his throat and shook his head.

"Please, have a seat. She's had a sedative, so she'll probably be out for the remainder of the evening."

"That's understandable. Will you let her know I stopped by to check on her?"

"I sure will, and thanks again for stopping by," he said, while escorting her to the door.

"Have a good evening." Samantha walked out feeling a bit uncomfortable.

As soon as Robert was sure she was down the hall and out of sight, he retrieved his phone, punched some numbers on the keypad, and turned his back to the entrance.

Staring out the window, he said, "We need to talk. It's urgent. When will you be back in town?" he asked before pausing. "Call me the minute you hit Turner," he said sharply before slamming the phone it its holster. Then he started mumbling and pacing back and forth in the room as Sheretta laid in the bed.

When he heard a knock on the closed door, he rushed over to keep the visitor from waking Sheretta. After opening the door, he stood in silence.

"I'm sorry. I almost forgot I had a book for Sheretta. I know she loves to read. She talks about her book club all the time," Samantha whispered, handing him the book.

"Um...thanks. I'll make sure she gets it."

As he returned to the window, his mind seemed to be lost in the clouds. He stared out the glass into space. The stars were visible, but this beautiful night held a mystery of its own.

*****

As Samantha walked into her spacious apartment, she kicked off her heels at the door and made her way to the bedroom. Before throwing her clothes on the chair that often doubled as a closet, she put them to her nose in order to get another smell of the man that she'd fallen for. Then she stepped in the shower.

"I love this new body cream," Samantha said as she slipped on her gown and housecoat. "I can tell a difference in my skin already. I don't know who Clarice is, but I love Azure. She definitely knows what a sister needs."

After going into the kitchen and pulling a salad from the fridge, she ate and made her way to the cozy living room.

"I think I'll give Mr. Chase a call before it gets too late, or should I make him wait a day or two?" Samantha sniffed his business card and smiled. "Even the business card says rich," she chuckled.

Meanwhile, Daryl Chase was on the phone in a nearby Charleston hotel suite. "Yes, I've made contact. You know I'm smooth." He laughed. "Speaking of her, she's beeping in now. I'll talk to you tomorrow," he said and then clicked over.

Raging Storms *(Part 2)*

"Hello, Daryl Chase speaking."

"Hello, Mr. Chase. This is Samantha. We met earlier at the convenience store."

"I'd know that voice of yours anywhere. I was just thinking about you," he responded.

"Oh, you were, were you? And just what were you thinking?"

"I was thinking about how fortunate I was to have met such a beautiful woman."

"Thank you for those kind words. First, I'd like to thank you for paying for the gas. I really feel bad about it. It was my fault; I should have been paying attention."

"Don't worry about the gas. I should have been watching the pump," he replied. "I thought you'd forgotten all about me," he teased, leaning back on the bed with his hands behind his head.

"How could I ever forget a gentleman such as yourself?"

"I thought a woman as beautiful as you would be taken, so I assumed you'd never call."

"If I wasn't going to call, or if I was taken—as you call it, I wouldn't have accepted your business card in the first place," Samantha responded as she looked at her bright red toes and wiggled them. "Well, Mr. Chase, just what brought you to Turner, and how long will you be with us?"

"Let's just say I'll be around for a while." He stood and walked across the room to stare out the window. "Enough about me; I want to know more about you," he said before taking a sip of his drink.

"I'm the oldest of eight children. My parents have lived in Turner their entire lives. I'm single and don't have any children."

"Where are you employed? Are you seeing anyone? Do you cook? Do you enjoy traveling?" He rattled out one question after another.

"Wow, you're thorough." Samantha sighed. "I'm employed at WeCumm Communications. No, I'm not seeing anyone at the moment. I love to cook, and I make it my business to travel every chance I get."

"What's your favorite food?" he asked.

"I love southern fried chicken. What about you?"

"I have two," he replied. "Lobster and shrimp are equally my absolute favorites."

"What a combination. Lobster and shrimp?" she said before lowering her music.

"Yes," he continued. "I'm a different type of man. Very unusual if I must say so myself."

"I see. I like unusual. I'm a bit unusual myself. Out of all of my siblings, I'm the one that's different from the rest. I guess it's because I'm the oldest."

"What makes you different?" he asked.

"I guess you'd have to see us together. I'm outspoken; they're all passive. I love to travel to exotic places, while they're content just being right here in little old Turner. I can't describe all of the differences."

"Well, all I know is I'd like to get to know you better," he said. "I tell you what, I'll be back in Turner in a few days. Let's say we do dinner."

Samantha laughed. "You really don't know much about Turner, do you? There's not a single place that you can find decent lobster and shrimp in this town."

"Well, I guess we'll have to do Charleston. I know several spots that have wonderful food. We might even find some southern fried chicken," he teased.

"Do you have something to write with?"

"Yes, I do." He walked over and picked up the pad and pencil from the hotel desk.

"My name is Samantha Sharpe and my number is 843-111-1189."

"Okay, I've stored it in my phone. Have a good night, and we'll talk tomorrow. Rest well, my dear."

"Goodnight, Mr. Chase."

"Please, call me Daryl."

"Goodnight, Daryl."

Samantha was as giddy as a sixteen-year-old going out on her first date. She couldn't wait to call her best friend Sandy and tell her about her handsome new acquaintance. They talked for hours before Sandy fell asleep on the phone, and Samantha ended up hanging up on her.

*****

"Good morning, Mama. I was going to call you last night, but it was late when I got home and settled," Samantha lied. "I wanted to let you know that I was going to be the interim accounting supervisor while Sheretta Miller is recuperating."

"Lord have mercy. I heard about her accident. How's she doing?" Laura Sharpe asked. "Her accident has been the talk of the town over the last couple of days. I know her family is worried; they're a close-knit family. I bet her father will be here any day."

"She's hanging in there. I've been going to the hospital to check on her every day. And, Mama, her dad's already here. I met him at the hospital."

Laura paused. "It's been years since I've seen him. He was something way back when. He was one good-looking man. He always thought he was God's gift to society, but his sister Lucy was just the sweetest person you'd ever want to meet. Over the years, we lost contact. Lucy rarely ever leaves their family farm."

"Well, to tell you the truth, he acted strange, like....I don't know, just strange. Mama, I can't be late for work. I'll call you tonight. I love you."

"Oh, okay, baby. I love you, too. I'm just glad she survived. Did you remember that Sheretta had her accident on the last day of September?"

"Mom, I almost forgot."

As Laura Sharpe sat on the edge of the bed, her mind traveled back thirty-nine years. Her plump, round face was just as pretty today as it was when she was seventeen years old. She remembered her parents and the financial struggles they faced, as well as the decision that was made for her that would change her life forever.

"God, I just want to thank you for blessing me to make it after all I've been through. I may never understand why things happened like they did, but I trust you, Lord."

She wept as she dressed. When she finished, she went to the bathroom, wiped her face, and dabbed her eyes with a cool cloth before going into the kitchen to prepare breakfast.

*****

"Good morning, Mr. McCall," Samantha greeted as she walked inside WeCumm ten minutes early.

"Good morning, Samantha. Are you ready for the big move?" he asked. "You look nice."

"Thank you for the compliment, and, yes, it shouldn't take too long because everything is boxed and ready to go."

"I placed Sheretta's belongings in boxes and put them in the locked storage cabinet," Mr. McCall informed Samantha. "I went to see her the other day, and she'd been moved out of intensive care and onto a unit. Poor thing, she's broken up pretty bad. I heard her uppity father was in town."

"I met him at the hospital. He's different. He looks at people like they're trash or something," Samantha commented.

"He's been that way since childhood. Him and his family think they're more than they are. Those brothers of his have always been womanizers. From what I hear, he's been asking questions around town."

"Questions about what?" asked Samantha.

"The rumor around town is that he has some hare brain idea that this was no ordinary accident."

"He's crazy. In a town the size of Turner, where everybody knows everybody, who would even think such a thing?"

"You're right. Who would do such a thing on purpose?" he asked while heading for the door.

"All set," said Samantha as she settled in the chair behind the desk. "I'm going to get to work."

"Well, I'm going to let you get started. This office has been vacant for days, so I'm sure you have a lot of catching up to do."

"Okay. Thanks for everything, Samantha said, then mumbled, "I've got to show Ms. Hardy that I can do this job better than Sheretta."

Ding-dong! Samantha looked at her cell phone. It was a text from Daryl, which read, *Good morning. I hope you a have a beautiful day. Thinking of you...Daryl.*

A smile as broad as the Little River crossed Samantha's face as she sent him a return text.

Thank you. I'm looking forward to talking to you soon, she typed and then pressed send.

"Mr. Sorenson, this is Samantha Sharpe. I'll be taking over for Sheretta Miller while she's out. I wanted to let you know if you have any questions or concerns, I'm a phone call away."

"Thank you, young lady. I read about her accident in the paper. I hope she'll be fine," he said. "I'm going to have my secretary send her some flowers."

"Flowers would be nice. I've been checking on her. She's got a rough road ahead, and from what I hear, she's going to need physical therapy once she's released."

"Well, thank you for your call. I'm sure we'll be fine until Sheretta's return. Have a good day."

"Yes, sir. We'll work well together. Thank you, and you have a good day, as well."

A tap on the open door took Samantha's attention from the contract she was revising.

"Come in," she said as she removed her glasses, placed them on her desk, and looked toward the door.

"Samantha, these are for you," said Tony, placing a huge bouquet of flowers on her desk.

"Thanks, Tony. Please close the door on your way out. My mother is spoiling me again."

The arrangement was breathtaking, but larger than the flowers her mother had sent in the past. The deep purple vase was exquisite. The purple roses, lavender alstroemeria, white lilies, and purple stock flowers were simply gorgeous. The card read, *I can't stop thinking about you… Daryl.*

"Wow, this man is different."

Samantha picked up her phone, searched the contact listing for Daryl's number, and pressed the button to dial.

"Hello," answered Daryl.

"Daryl, this is Samantha. I wanted to call and thank you for the flowers. They're beautiful," she said before taking a whiff of the card that bore his distinct scent.

It was obvious he'd handled the card. A whiff of the arrangement that covered a portion of the desk sent her mind in imaginary fairytale mode.

"A beautiful lady such as yourself deserves nothing but the best." He paused. "Don't you agree?"

"Yes, and thanks again. This is a special day for me, and I am elated that you'd think of me."

"Well, I'm happy I was able to add joy to your day. Tell me, how is your special day going so far?" he asked.

"Today's my first day in a new position."

"Congratulations. A new position deserves a celebration," he chimed as he pulled his sunglasses from his head and changed lanes. "I wasn't coming back to Turner until later in the week, but schedules are made to be altered. We must do dinner."

"That sounds lovely. Although, I must remind you that there's no place in Turner that has lobster and shrimp." Samantha chuckled.

"Won't you be exhausted after your first day on a new job?" he asked.

"Well, actually, I've been with the company for years, so what I'm doing is nothing new." She paused before adding, "The girl I'm replacing had an accident."

"Well, in that case, I'll be finished around four. What time is good for you?"

"I get off at five, so how about six o'clock?"

"Sounds good," Daryl replied. "I know this quaint place in Charleston that has almost everything we like. Where can I pick you up?"

"I'll text my address to you since you're driving."

"How do you know I'm driving?" he asked.

"Because I hear horns blowing in the background."

"You're a sharp young lady. I'll see you around six," he told her. "At dinner, you can tell me about your position."

"It's a date. I'll see you later, and thanks again," she said before ending the call.

As she sat at her desk reminiscing about their encounter yesterday, she wondered where Daryl Chase had been all her life.

The remainder of the day was spent making contact with account holders in reference to customer service issues, reviewing accounts to make sure payments were coming in and being processed on time, contacting delinquent account holders, and submitting proposals to potential new clients. Every so often, Samantha's mind would drift back to Daryl Chase. Before she knew anything it was five after five. She gathered her things and hurried out.

"Oh my, I'm home with less than fifty minutes to shower and dress," said Samantha to herself as she ran through her bathroom. "I'll wear this purple and black dress. It does it every time."

Forty-five minutes later, the sound of the doorbell caused her heart to race. She slipped on her black stilettos and opened the door.

"Hello. You look fabulous," Daryl complimented as he stood in awe.

His black suit, crisp white shirt with black diamond cufflinks, platinum watch with floating diamonds, and horn-toed shoes that had been polished to perfection definitely said rich.

"You were cute yesterday, but you're absolutely fabulous tonight."

"Thank you," Samantha replied, slightly blushing. "You look spiffy yourself. So...where are we going?"

"We're going to a spot in Charleston called The Crest. They serve the best food around," he told her.

Daryl held her coat as she eased into it, made sure her front door was locked, escorted her to the passenger side, opened the door, and held her hand as she slid in. He then closed the door and walked around to the driver's side.

"So, Samantha, tell me about this new position of yours and how your first day went."

"I'm the interim accounting supervisor for commercial accounts at WeCumm Communications. I'll be replacing a coworker who's been in an automobile accident."

"Is she going to be alright?" he asked.

"I'm not sure. I've been to visit, but I don't really know the extent of her injuries."

The ride was relaxing; the conversation was refreshing. It was as if they'd known each other for years.

"Here we are, The Crest. Here you'll find the best food in the area," he said while maneuvering the black sports car into the valet parking area.

The valet opened her door, and Daryl escorted her to the restaurant.

"Samantha, you look lovely."

"Thank you, Daryl. You do, too," Samantha replied as she looked at him and smiled, causing her right dimple to be excessively visible.

The Crest reminded her of a restaurant she'd seen while vacationing in New York several years ago. The front of the establishment housed huge potted ferns on each side of the entrance. A stained glass window with a rainbow and calming blue water at the base covered the front left side of the building, while a red carpet covered by a red awning leading to the front door and a doorman waiting for patrons captured her attention.

Once inside, the rustic yet elegant decor rendered her speechless. Six columns flanked the spacious foyer, while vintage paintings gave it charm. The furniture and accent pieces provided elegance, ambiance, and hints of personalization. The reputation of The Crest had surfaced in Turner, but not many residents were able to afford such a place, or even thought of such an adventure as a necessity.

After being seated and looking over the menu, Samantha was spellbound. Growing up as one of eight children, she always had what was needed, but spending frivolously was out of the question.

"Samantha, what would you like for dinner?" Daryl asked, looking across the table. "They have a delicious wine-baked chicken with caramelized potatoes and green beans that I hear is quite tasty," he added. "It's not southern fried chicken, but I'm sure you'll like it."

"Everything sounds delicious."

"Trust me, the food is magnificent," he said as the waiter approached their table.

"Good evening, Mr. Chase. Welcome to The Crest. My name is Wallace, and I will be serving you. May I suggest a wine for either of you this evening?"

"I'm going to pass," Daryl responded. "I'd like some iced tea with pure lemon juice, please."

"And for you, ma'am?" asked Wallace as he directed his attention to Samantha.

Samantha skimmed the menu and then looked at the waiter. "I'd like to try your strawberry lemonade with fresh strawberries. It sounds refreshing."

"Mr. Chase, can I start you out with any appetizers?"

"Yes, Wallace, I'd like to start with some Cajun shrimp dip," Daryl said, while placing the menu on the table and casting his eyes on Samantha. "For my main entrée, I'd like the steamed lobster, shrimp sautéed in butter sauce, with seasoned corn on the cob and herbal potatoes."

The waiter looked at Samantha as she looked at the menu as if she were studying for an exam. She finally looked up and smiled.

"I would like the shrimp and grits as an appetizer. I'd also like to try the wine-baked chicken and caramelized potatoes and asparagus."

Wallace nodded. "Yes, ma'am. I'll be back shortly."

"Samantha, what do you think of The Crest so far?"

"It's lovely. The atmosphere is quite relaxing. It's like Paris in South Carolina." She chuckled. "As if I'd ever been to Paris."

"I'm glad you like it."

"You must be a regular, Daryl. The waiter called you by name."

"No, I'm actually from North Carolina. From time to time, I'm here on business."

"What business are you in?"

"Let's just stay, it's the family business. Tonight, I want to hear all about you, Samantha Sharpe," he said as he looked past Samantha toward the front entrance.

"On one condition," Samantha responded.

He laughed. "And what's that?"

"I'll tell you about me if you'll do the same, Daryl Chase."

"Deal."

"Where do I start? I'm just a country girl. I'm the oldest of eight. I've lived in Turner my whole life. I'm a graduate of Central Community College and have a degree in Accounting."

"I don't take you as just a country girl. You carry yourself in a way that exemplifies taste, character, and sophistication."

"Why, thank you."

"Where are your parents?" he asked.

"They're in Turner. My mom just retired and my dad still works. He should be retiring in a couple of years. He's the type of man who thinks a man should work until he takes his last breath. Besides, if he retires, he'd be bored stiff." She smiled. "My parents are hardworking people who've provided for their children, and at the same time, they taught us the value of being hard workers."

"Here you are, ma'am, strawberry lemonade with fresh strawberries, and for you, sir, iced tea with pure lemon juice," said Wallace as he placed the drinks on the table. "I'll be back. Enjoy your beverages."

After taking a sip of her drink, Samantha smiled and cast her eyes on Daryl. "This is delicious. It's sweet just like I like it."

"I'm glad you're enjoying it."

"Now, the one thing I am is fair. I've told you all about me; now, it's your turn," she said as she looked across the table past the fresh flowers nestled in a short crystal vase. "Where are you from and why did you grace the good folks of Turner with your presence?"

Daryl wiped his mouth with the linen napkin, placed it on the table, and said, "There's not much to tell. I'm the middle child; I have three brothers and a sister. My sister is the oldest. My parents are from North Carolina. Despite objections from my great-grandfather, my parents decided to migrate to New York immediately after graduating and getting married. They had aspirations of making it big in The Big Apple. When my great-grandfather passed, they moved back to help run the family business. The two youngest were still at home with my parents, so they had no choice but to return to North Carolina."

"Wow, you have an interesting life. What was it like growing up in the big city?" Samantha asked, her eyes expanding.

"New York is not as bad as people make it out to be. My sister, the spoiled fashion queen, decided New York was where she wanted to be, so she stayed. After graduating from college, I worked in corporate America for ten years. I loved my job and the salary was nice. Just when I was up for another promotion, my grandmother became ill, and my brothers who had all moved north had no interest whatsoever in relocating to North Carolina. So, me being single, I decided it would be easier for me to make the move. There's really not that much to tell," he said as he sat back in the chair, took a sip of iced tea, and looked across the table at Samantha.

"How is your grandmother?" Samantha asked.

Daryl chuckled. "She is one tough lady. She bounced back in less than six months. She still drives everywhere she wants to go and works closely with the daily operations of the business."

"That's amazing."

A broad smile covered Daryl's face as he shook his head. "You know what? She's amazing. It took my parents three months to pack up and take my two younger brothers back to North Carolina. Less than two months after my parents moved back home, my grandmother suddenly got better. To this day, my mother believes Grandmother's illness was all a ploy to get my father back on North Carolina soil."

Time vanished as they enjoyed each other's company. The meal was everything Daryl said it would be. It was obvious, because Samantha's plate contained only remnants of the meal. The restaurant was almost empty when Samantha just happened to look around.

"Daryl, you were right. The food was magnificent. Thank you for a wonderful evening," she said as they left the restaurant.

"You're welcome. It was my pleasure."

During the ride home, they laughed and talked like they'd known each other for years. When Samantha eyed the town of Turner sign, she acted as if she was Cinderella and the clock was striking midnight. Her face was evident of her feelings.

"Daryl, thanks again for a wonderful evening. This is the most fun I've had in quite some time," she said, while looking over at him.

The night was dark, but with the aid of lighting from other vehicles, she could see just how handsome he was.

"It was indeed my pleasure."

When Daryl stopped the car, Samantha clinched her purse, not wanting the night to end. She inhaled as she closed her eyes for a second and allowed her nose to enjoy his scent. The scent she'd grown to love captured her emotions.

Daryl eased her door open, extended his hand, and broke her out of her daydream.

When Samantha's hand met his, a tingle ran down her spine. She felt a feeling she hadn't felt in quite some time.

"Daryl, thanks again. I'll call you later in the week," she told him, then hurried up the steps in order to keep her sanity and something else.

"Goodnight and thanks for a wonderful evening," he said as he stood on the porch and waited to see her safely inside.

As Samantha readied herself for bed, she thought about her date and the attentiveness of Daryl Chase.

*****

"Good morning, Mr. McCall," greeted Samantha as she entered the WeCumm building.

"Well, hello, Samantha. You're here mighty early," Mr. McCall said as he hurried past her.

"I've got a full day, so I thought I'd get an early start," she replied.

When she looked around, she realized he was nowhere in sight. Upon entering her office, she noticed the door was unlocked.

"I could've sworn I locked the door," she muttered. "Oh well, let me get busy. I have so much to do."

As Samantha went about her daily duties, she couldn't help thinking about the wonderful evening she had.

*****

Daryl stood in the hotel lobby on his cell phone and admired the scenery as he waited for the valet to bring his car around.

"We had dinner here in Charleston last night. Everything's going according to plan. I'll call you next week and give you another update." He paused. "I promise you, she has no idea," he continued, then listened to the voice on the other end of the line. "Okay, I've got things to do. I'll keep you posted. I'm heading to Turner, so I've got to get going," he said before ending the call.

*****

Monroe sat in silence as he read the report from the Charleston police department. He slammed the manila folder on the edge of the metal desk and stood to his feet.

"How could this have happened? Evidence shouldn't just disappear from a police station evidence room," yelled Monroe, then plopped back down in the chair facing Captain Pierce.

"Calm down. Remember, as long as you keep a level head, you'll remain focused and be able to solve this case," Captain Pierce said as he sat observing the actions of one of the best officers he'd ever worked with.

"How can you tell me that the tires on the car that tried to kill Sheretta cannot be traced?" he blurted out.

"Monroe, I think you need to take a step back and let us handle the investigation from here on out. The chief wants to meet with me in the morning." Captain Pierce sat up and looked in Monroe's eyes. "I tell you what. You focus on taking care of Sheretta and leave this case to us."

"I need to work this case," Monroe commanded.

"Sorry, Tate. I didn't want to tell you, but I got orders from the chief. You're officially off this case."

"What do you mean, I'm off this case?" Monroe asked, standing to his feet. "I'll just see about that." He stormed out into the corridor and walked down the halls of the old musty building.

After knocking one time, he burst into the chief's office and yelled, "Chief, Captain Pierce just informed me that you've ordered me off the case." Before he could say another word, he looked to his left and saw Robert Miller sitting across from the chief. "I should have known you had something to do with this," he blurted out. "This is all about you."

"Officer Tate, that's enough," said Chief Tucker as he moved from his desk and proceeded to close his office door. "I'm going to excuse you this time, but let me make this crystal clear. You are under my command, and as long as I'm the chief, you'll do exactly what I say. Do you understand?"

"Monroe, I was just asking the chief to help find out what happened," Robert Miller said with a smirk on his face.

"When will you ever stop throwing your weight around? You just don't think I'm good enough for your daughter. Why don't you admit it?" he shouted.

"Tate, if you cannot conduct yourself as an officer of the law, I'm going to ask you to leave," warned Chief Tucker as he walked over to Monroe and stood just inches from his face.

Monroe turned and stormed out without so much as another word.

"Sheretta, I didn't believe you before, but now I do," Monroe mumbled.

His grip on the steering wheel tightened. He gnawed the inside of his jaw and drove recklessly through town as if he was on the Charlotte Motor Speedway.

"Tate, calm down. Tate, calm down," he repeated to himself.

Before he knew anything, he was pulling into a parking space at the hospital.

"Well, hello," said an elderly lady sitting in a wheelchair inside the hospital doors at the front entrance with her belongings in her lap.

"Hello, Mother Gray. Pastor Walters told us that you were in here," said Monroe as he stopped, removed his sunglasses, and gave her a kiss on her cheek. "How are you?"

"Baby, I'm blessed. Them old doctors said I'd have to stay here a week. I told them I'm a praying woman and that I'd be going home sooner," she stated with a chuckle. "Look at God. I'm going home after four days. God sure is good. Look, baby, I heard about Sheretta's accident. I've been praying for her. How's she doing?" she asked.

"Mother Gray, she's doing just fine. After a few more days, she'll be going home, as well."

"Praise God, baby. My son is here. I'm going on home so I can watch that big-screen television my grandchildren got me for my birthday." She laughed.

"Hello," said Mother Gray's son as he walked over and shook Monroe's hand.

"Hi, how are you? Your mother is a testimony," Monroe commented.

"She sure is, and we thank Him for her daily," he responded as he looked toward the sky.

"Mother Gray, take care." Monroe said, then shook Mother Gray's son's hand once again and helped her into his car.

Walking the halls of Turner Memorial was never dull. The elderly gentleman struggled to hold his IV pole and keep his gown closed, but he managed to carry his cigarettes. Monroe shook his head. A young woman in her late teens walked the halls in yellow pajamas. Obviously not a patient, she had her handbag in one hand and a young boy clenched the other hand. When Monroe rounded the corner to the unit, he nodded at a smiling Nurse McQueen as she flipped charts at the nurse's station.

As usual, Sheretta was sound asleep.

"I'm here, baby," Monroe whispered.

As he sat in his usual spot in the corner, he flipped out his phone and began jotting down some of the details he would need to investigate Sheretta's accident now that he had one less clue to work with. He had only been in her room about twenty minutes when her dad appeared. His jaw tightened, and he stared at him as if he was the enemy.

"Monroe, can I see you outside for a moment?" he whispered.

Without so much as a word, Monroe rushed out into the hall.

"Monroe, despite what you may think, I had nothing to do with the chief's decision."

"If you think for one minute I believe that, you've got to be crazy," he said between clenched teeth. "You know what? Contrary to what you might think, everything is not about you."

"My only concern is the well-being and safety of my Sheretta. After you stormed out, the chief and I had a long talk, and I owe you an apology," he offered.

Monroe froze with a blank stare on his face.

Robert Miller continued. "I want you to know I believe you love Sheretta and you only want what's best for her."

"Yes, sir, I do. I only want to take care of her and make her happy."

"Truce," said Robert as he extended his hand.

"Truce," said Monroe, while extending his hand to shake with the man who he still had his doubts about.

*****

They re-entered the room to find me flipping channels on the television.

105

"Where have you two been? I've got good news. The doctor is releasing me. I can go home tomorrow. My physical therapy starts next week," I said, while looking from one to the other. "What have you two been up to?

"Let's just say we had a man to man," replied my dad as he smiled at Monroe.

"I'm going to need you two to go home so you can be here bright and early. I'm ready to go home and get settled."

"Well, she's given us orders, so I think we're supposed to follow them," teased Monroe.

"Goodnight, Princess. We'll see you in the morning."

*****

They walked the corridor, and for the first time, the two of them actually had a civil conversation that wasn't strained.

"Monroe, I'll meet you here at nine or so, and we'll take Sheretta home and get her settled in. If that's okay with you, of course."

"That sounds like a plan. I want to be here when the doctor discharges her so I can make sure her physical therapy appointments are scheduled," said Monroe.

"Good idea. You're going to make a great son-in-law after all."

"Thank you. I'll see you in the morning," Monroe said just before walking out to the parking lot.

THREE WEEKS LATER...

"Samantha, this has been the longest month ever," said Daryl, while staring out at the morning sun.

His master bedroom was on the east of his estate, and it was as if each ray of sun was at his command.

Samantha laughed. "It's only been three weeks. Daryl, when you said you'd be returning to North Carolina, I had no idea I'd think of you so often," she admitted. "When will you be returning? I know Turner's Cafe is no match for The Crest, but our next dinner will be my treat. I've truly enjoyed the times we've spent together."

"I should be back tomorrow. Trust me, I have had the time of my life with you. Do you remember when we both fell asleep at the movies holding hands?" he asked. "Dinner anyplace sounds good as long as you'll be there with me."

"Awww, you're sweet, and don't remind me. That's a sign we're getting old," she teased.

Samantha turned to her computer so she could begin checking emails, sending out bids, and returning phone calls from clients.

"Have a good day, darling. I've got another call. I'll see you tomorrow," he said before clicking over on his cell to begin his next conversation.

"Hello. I've been meaning to return your calls," said Daryl. After a brief pause, he continued. "I know what my mission was. I have some doubts about the assignment."

He paused again, removed the phone from his ear, and peered at it, while the person on the other end yelled.

"After time and thought, I really think you've made a big mistake," Daryl continued. "I've had the opportunity to get to know her, so I've decided to decline your offer."

Daryl then disconnected the call. His cell began to ring. After looking at the display, he hurled it across the room and cradled his head in his hands.

*****

The presence of someone in her doorway stole her attention.

"Hello, Samantha. How are things? How much longer are you going to be here this afternoon?"

"I'm so happy, Mr. McCall. Things seem so unreal. I've met the man of my dreams, and all of my years of hard work are finally paying off," replied Samantha. "I'll be packing up soon. This job is a breeze," she continued.

"That's great. I told you this was supposed to be your job," Mr. McCall said as he looked out the corner of his eye. "Have you heard how Sheretta is coming along?" Samantha inquired.

"No. What's been going on?" he asked.

"You know I've been stopping by to see her regularly. She's still taking physical therapy. Sometimes she goes to the rehabilitation unit and sometimes the therapist goes to her house. She said she hopes to be back at work soon. You know, since I left Mount Pisgah, things have been better." Samantha paused and looked at Mr. McCall.

"My son and his family have joined there, and they love it," Deacon McCall interjected.

"I know. I see those handsome grandsons of yours at church. Deliverance Temple is rocking."

"I'd leave if it wasn't for my wife. She's Pastor Walters' cousin, and she refuses to leave." He blew breath from his mouth and shook his head.

"Well, have a good evening. I'm going to see Sheretta this afternoon when I get off. Tomorrow I have plans, so I'd better go by to check on her. I'll let you know if anything changes."

"Okay. I'll wait for your report Monday morning."

*****

The driveway was full when Samantha arrived. "Sheretta must have company. I wonder who it is?" she said to herself as she put the car in gear, snatched her pocketbook from the seat, jumped out, and rushed to the front door.

Tap...Tap...

Seconds later, she could hear the locks jiggling as someone tried to open the huge wooden door.

"Hello, can I help you?" asked the man who she remembered to be Sheretta's father.

"Hello, Mr. Miller. I'm—" she attempted before being interrupted.

"Yes, come in. You're Sheretta's coworker, Samantha Sharpe."

"Thank you," said Samantha as she walked in and stopped just inside the door. "I just came to check on Sheretta to see how she's recuperating. I see you have company. I don't want to bother you."

"She's upstairs in bed. I'd hate to wake her. She's been having some rough nights. Come, please have a seat," said Robert as he walked into the living room and sat on the sofa. "My rental car is acting up. So, they dropped me off a new one but haven't gotten around to having the other one towed as of yet."

"Well, I hate to bother you."

"No bother. I'd like to speak with you for just a minute."

Despite her reluctance, Samantha moved over to the chair and sat down. "Yes, sir, what is it that you'd like to speak with me about?" she asked, narrowing her eyes.

"May I call you Samantha, Ms. Sharpe?" he asked as he removed his cufflinks and loosened his tie.

"Yes, sir, that would be fine."

"I hear you're filling in for Sheretta while she's recuperating. During the last few weeks, she's been through quite a bit. First, the trouble at work with the likes of Kyle Carroll, then the accident, then physical therapy, and now the restless nights. My question to you is how do you think the pressures of this new job will affect her?" he asked, moving to the edge of the sofa.

"What do you mean?" Samantha asked with wide eyes.

"You've been doing the job. Will it be too much for my princess?" he asked.

"In my honest opinion, yes, it will. I work long hours, and sometimes I'm forced to take work home in order to keep up."

"Thank you, young lady. That's just what I've been thinking," he said before standing. "Thank you very much for your time. I won't bother you anymore. By the way, you look familiar. Have you been in Turner long?" Robert asked, already knowing the answer to that question.

"Yes, I've lived here all my life," she said as she stood. "My parents are Laura and Robert Sharpe. You probably don't remember them," she added, remembering how her mother spoke of Robert Miller.

"Okay, thanks again," he said, then turned to walk to the door. "One more thing, I'd like to keep this little chat between us," he said just before clearing his throat. "I wouldn't want my princess' business floating all over town, if you know what I mean."

"Yes, sir, I understand. I won't say a word," she said, while walking down the steps at a brisk pace.

"I appreciate that, and again, thank you for your time." He watched her slide inside her car.

"There's something weird about that man," she mumbled as she picked up her cell and drove out of the neighborhood. After dialing her mother's number, she hung up after the first ring. "He did ask me to keep this quiet," she reminded herself.

*****

"Daddy, who were you talking to?" I asked as I came down the steps with my cane.

"Princess, what are you doing up? The doctor said you need your rest," Dad said, rushing to the base of the steps and reaching for my hand.

110

"Thank you, Daddy. I'm getting my rest. I'm going to talk to the doctor about taking me off some of the medications."

"Princess, why don't you think about coming back to New York with me for a few weeks?"

"You know I can't do that, Daddy. I need to get back to work. My house is a mess; I haven't been to church in weeks; and I know my work is piling up on me. I can't even think about going to New York," I snapped.

"Princess, those things you just mentioned can be taken care of. I can get your aunt to come and clean up; Pastor Walters has been coming by praying with you; and WeCumm will be just fine. While you're in New York, you can stay in the guesthouse next door. You'll be just seconds away from your family. I haven't used the guesthouse since I left the practice and went to the bench. There are three bedrooms and three bathrooms. You won't even have to cook. You can have your meals with us. Heck, you can go to Martin Memorial with us every Sunday."

"You know your precious wife doesn't like me nor does she want me around. She made that clear when I was ten," I added.

"She likes you," he said. "Sheretta, that was then; this is now. She'd love for you to come back with me."

"I've got to get back to work, and you know I hardly ever see Aunt Lucy, much less would I ask her to clean my house."

"Well, I'll hire a cleaning service to come in. We'll clean the house and lock it up. I know Monroe will take care of it."

"Daddy, that's a waste of money," I argued.

"Money is no object. I want you back in New York. That way, we can keep an eye on you. Your brothers and sisters are as concerned about you as I am."

"Please give me some time to think about it. Besides, I don't want to leave Monroe," I said, rubbing my irritated eyes.

"Stop rubbing your eyes. We'll talk about it later," he retreated.

"Who were you talking to earlier?" I asked for the second time.

"It was your co-worker Samantha Sharpe. She's a very nice young lady. I remember her mother. Laura was a little younger than me, but we went to school together. Her parents rented some land on the farm next to ours."

"Did Samantha say what she wanted? I bet she needs my help with something at work. I'll give her a call after dinner."

"Good idea, Princess. I just bet things are fine at WeCumm. Oh, I almost forgot. Monroe called and said he's working tonight, but he'll see you tomorrow."

"Why didn't you wake me up?" I asked, reaching for my cell phone. I dialed his number, but got his voicemail. "Monroe must be busy. He'll see my number and call back. Daddy, something smells good."

"I baked some beef ribs. I went to Lucy's while you were at physical therapy, and she had cooked cabbage, fresh corn on the cob, and macaroni and cheese. She sent me out of there with enough food for a week." He laughed. "She even told me to come back tomorrow. She's going to fix a big pot of chicken pastry and candied yams. She knows those are two of your favorites."

"Please tell her thank you. After dinner, I'll wash the dishes."

"I'll take care of the dishes. You need your rest. You definitely won't be washing any dishes tonight, young lady. Daddy's here," he said, then walked over and kissed me on the forehead

"I'm going to be spoiled if you keep this up."

"That's what dads are for."

"I'm going to take my meds and get some rest. Goodnight, Daddy."

"Goodnight, Princess. We'll talk more about New York in the morning."

"Okay."

*****

While preparing for bed, Samantha thought back to the conversation she'd had earlier with Robert Miller. There was something both familiar and unsettling, but she couldn't put her finger on it.

"Before I go to sleep, I need to hear your voice," she said as she dialed Daryl's number.

"Hello, and why aren't you asleep?" he asked.

"I just needed to hear your voice," she purred.

"Guess what?" he chimed. "I couldn't wait. After talking with you earlier, I realized I couldn't wait another minute. I needed to see you as soon as possible. I'm in Charleston. So, I'll see you in the morning."

"You are so thoughtful. I missed you, too."

"Samantha, tomorrow is Saturday, and I've got something special planned. I'll pick you up at eight. Goodnight, my love."

"Goodnight, Daryl. I—"

"Hello...hello...hello!" Daryl screamed without any response. "Samantha, answer me. Are you alright?" he asked before the line went dead.

He dialed the number back what seemed like a thousand times, with no answer each time.

"I know he didn't do it!" he screamed, while gripping the steering wheel and driving like never before.

More Storms

"My phone is dead. Ugh! I forgot my battery charger in my desk at work. I can't go the whole weekend without my phone. I'll just have to purchase another charger in the morning," Samantha said while taking her allergy medicine and clicking the switch on the light. As she covered her head with the comforter, she thought to herself, *Daryl, I'll call you first thing in the morning.* Then she closed her eyes.

"My God, please protect her. She's the best thing that's happened to me in over ten years. She's just got to be okay. If he hurt her, I'll kill him," Daryl swore as he drove like a pure madman.

Samantha slept through the sounds of night. Neither the dogs howling, trashcans that were being knocked over, or the sounds from the ambulances and fire trucks whizzing through the streets woke her from her coma-like slumber.

Meanwhile, Daryl had hit the city limits of Turner, only to see emergency service vehicles passing him at an alarming rate of speed.

"Samantha, I love you," he cried.

Two blocks from her home, he was stopped by a road block.

As he rolled down the window, he saw flames shooting across the bluish gray sky. Shifting the car into park, he shut the ignition off, stared out the window, and opened the door.

An officer on the scene saw him getting out of his car and told him, "Sir, you need to move on. We're in the process of evacuating the area."

"Officer, a friend of mine lives two streets over. I need to make sure she's alright," he pleaded with no success.

"Sir, I'm going to ask you to leave one more time. We've already had one known casualty. We're evacuating a two-block area."

"What's the address of the fire, officer? I need to know," he pleaded again.

"Sir, several residents have been transported to Turner Memorial. I cannot give any names until the next of kin has been notified," the officer replied firmly.

Daryl sat in the car with tears dripping from his eyes. He couldn't move. He sat as if he'd been paralyzed. His eyes were fixed and his heart raced, already knowing the fate of the woman he loved.

After another officer noticed the black car and driver, he walked over to the first officer to inquire. After a brief conversation, the officers looked in Daryl's direction and walked back over to the patrol car. As they observed Daryl, he looked up and saw them looking. Daryl wiped his eyes with a handkerchief and began to pray. The moment they began walking in his direction, a loud crash and piercing screams captured their attention.

Daryl backed out and headed in the direction of the city limits. When he arrived at his destination, he cut the ignition and cried as he did ten years ago when he lost the first woman he had intended to marry.

"What am I going to do?" Daryl cried.

He shifted into gear and drove irrationally until drained. When he realized anything, he was back in North Carolina on his estate, and it was three o'clock in the morning. Sitting in his car in his driveway, he reached in the glove compartment, removed his gun, and laid it in the empty seat next to him. He threw his head back and closed his eyes as tears escaped his eyes.

The next thing he heard was the ringing of his cell phone. Blinded by the morning sun, he shifted in his seat with closed eyes, looked at the unfamiliar number, and answered his cell.

"It's nine in the morning. What happened to you?" asked Samantha. "We've only been together a month and I've been stood up," she teased.

Daryl shot straight up in the seat. "Samantha, I tried to surprise you. After you hung up on me, I thought...Well, anyway, when I went to your neighborhood, a house was on fire and the police wouldn't let me through. All I saw were orange and red flames hovering the neighborhood," he rambled on.

"I know. When I woke up, the police were knocking on my door. I was the last person to be evacuated. I took my allergy medicine and it knocked me out," she told him. "I wasn't allowed to move my car, so Officer Tate took me to my parents' house in the patrol car. After I got here, my mom and dad were so grateful that we sat up and talked all night. The house three doors down caught on fire. Where have you been? It's been on the national news. It appears to have been arson. It's so sad, because the lady that lived there died in the fire."

"Samantha, we've got to talk. I've got something I need to tell you, but I need to do it in person. I'm a mess, though. I'm going to clean up, take a nap, and I'll see you this afternoon around three. Stay at your parents' place. Text me the address and I'll pick you up there," said Daryl just before telling her, "I love you, Samantha."

*****

News of the mysterious fire had Turner abuzz. It was as if Sheretta's accident happened decades ago. The front page of the newspaper was covered with the story of the suspicious blaze. Apparently, no one really knew the woman or where she was from. That itself was another mystery, because not much got by the nosey citizens of Turner.

"Sheretta, just look at this," said Robert Miller as he placed the newspaper in front of Sheretta so close that she had no choice but to read the horrific article. "This is confirmation that you need to be back in New York with me."

"Daddy, things happen in New York every day." She shook her head and rolled her eyes upward.

"Princess, please go back with me. If you stay until you get your health and strength back, I'll put you on a plane and send you back, no questions asked."

I sat without so much as saying a word. I hated New York and never wanted to be a burden on anyone.

"Daddy, I'm doing better. My house is clean again, and I'm moving much faster. Besides, Monroe is having an alarm installed. I'll be fine. I tell you what. If I feel like I can't handle it, I promise I'll call you and fly out to New York."

"You've always been tough, and I respect the fact that you're willing to try. I do see an improvement in your mobility, but I'll let you have your way on one condition." He paused. "You've always been daddy's girl and nothing will ever change that. But, if at any time you feel that you can't manage, you'll give me a call."

"Oh, Daddy, thank you so much. I promise, if I can't manage living here and taking care of things, you'll be the second to know. Of course, Daryl will be the first." I laughed.

"I still say you'd be the best attorney in the firm. You know how to win any argument." Dad laughed as he moved to the sofa.

*****

"Samantha, I'm so glad to see you." Daryl hugged her so tight she had to gasp for breath.

"Wow, I know it's been a while, but I'm here and I'm okay," she said as her parents stood in the doorway and watched.

"You don't have to worry about me ever leaving you again. I 'm making a promise to you," he told her with tremors in his voice.

"Daryl, come on. I want you to meet my parents. Mom, Dad, this is Daryl Chase."

"Nice to meet you, Mr. and Mrs. Sharpe. I've heard so much about you."

"Daryl, I've heard quite a bit about you, as well," responded Laura Sharpe as she smiled and embraced him with a gentle hug. "Welcome to our home."

"Thank you. I'm glad to have finally met you," he said. "Mr. Sharpe, it's nice to meet you, as well."

"Where'd you say you were from?" Robert Sharpe asked with a straight face.

"I'm from North Carolina, sir."

"How'd you say the two of you met again?" Mr. Sharpe's face bore a frown and his lips were pressed together.

"We met by accident at the gas station," said Daryl.

"Well, Daryl, it was nice meeting you. You're welcome here anytime."

"Thank you both, and it was nice to meet the two of you. Samantha goes on and on about you all the time."

Laura smiled. She knew Samantha was happy, and that was all that mattered.

"Mom and Dad, we'll be going now. I've inconvenienced you way too much already," said Samantha.

"This will always be your home. Y'all drive carefully. Are you going home or coming back here?" asked Laura. She stood so close to her husband that if you didn't know better, you'd think she was timid.

"Again, nice to meet you," said Daryl as he walked Samantha to her door.

Once he made sure she was inside and the door was closed, he walked around to the driver's side and then waved at the two as they stood on the porch.

After easing in and putting on his seatbelt, he looked over and said, "Your mom is a sweetheart."

"Yes, she is. My dad is nice, too. He just acts a bit funny when any of us bring home a guy. He's like any other fa-

ther. He only wants the best for his oldest angel." She chuckled.

"I know, but he was not feeling me."

Samantha laughed as she looked at Daryl.

"Why are you laughing?" He looked at her, awaiting an
answer. "Well...what's so funny?"

"Nothing. I just couldn't imagine you being intimidated."

"I'm not intimidated," he muffled as he maneuvered the
curves on the winding country road. "Anyway, you said dinner
was on you. You promised me some Turner cuisine, and I can't
wait."

"Again, it's not The Crest, but the food is delicious.
They have the best soups, burgers, and sandwiches in town,"
Samantha proclaimed.

"Well, how many restaurants do they have to compete
with?" he asked, turning the radio down.

"There are only three places to eat in town, but we
manage. The rumor is that the men and women of Turner can
out-cook any famous chef or restaurateur around," she bragged.
"Turn left here," she told him, pointing to the left.

"Well, I don't know about that. My family may not be
in South Carolina, but I've heard from a few folks that the
Chase family does pretty well in the kitchen," he boasted. "On
a serious note, we need to talk. I have something I got to tell
you," he said, while looking straight ahead as he drove through
the narrow streets of the quaint town.

"What is it, Daryl? You sound serious."

At that moment, Samantha's cell phone began to ring
and their conversation came to a halt.

"Hello..." Samantha paused. "This is she."

Samantha's eyes roamed and she appeared to be listening to the caller on the other end. After a few more seconds,
she ended the call without a goodbye or thank you.

"Is everything alright?" Daryl asked as he looked back and forth between her and the road.

"Yes, I'm fine. Daryl, what did you say you wanted to talk to me about?" she asked, looking in his direction and wringing her hands.

"It was nothing. Obviously the call disturbed you, and I need to know what's going on," he demanded, raising his voice.

"I'm fine. Let it go. It was just a call from someone from my past. It's nothing you need to be concerned with," she insisted.

In what seemed to be a nervous manner, she flattened her skirt and held the inside of her jaw with her teeth.

"Well, we'll talk later. I don't want anything to spoil our day. We've waited weeks for this, and nothing's going to ruin it." He reached over and caressed her hand.

"Daryl Chase, you need to keep both hands on the steering wheel," she said, forcing a laugh and a smile. "Turn left here, and Turner's Cafe is on your right."

"Well, here we are, the world famous Turner's Cafe," he said as he looked past Samantha out the window.

When he saw the unlit neon sign sporting the name of the establishment, he knew he'd arrived. As Daryl guided the car to the curb, he realized there were no large crowds, no parking meters, and no loitering. Everyone was going about their business in a calm, quiet manner.

"I could get use to a place like this," he mumbled.

"What did you say?"

"I was just thinking aloud," he answered. "You promised me a good meal, and that's what I'm expecting," he said just before jumping out of the car and rushing around to open the door.

They were met by stares from onlookers as they entered the rectangular brick building, which housed the fifteen or so patrons who were already occupying the establishment.

"Hello, Samantha," greeted the waitress dressed in black and white. Her voice was aiming at Samantha, but her eyes were locked on Daryl.

"Hello. We'd like to sit at a booth please," Samantha said in a tone that caught the flirtatious waitress' attention.

"Okay, you can sit there," she said, pointing to a booth near the picture window before returning to the register after noticing three people waiting to pay their bill.

"You certainly have her attention," Samantha commented.

He laughed and replied, "She's probably harmless."

"I'm not laughing." Samantha covered her face with the menu and looked at it as if she was scouring for gold.

"You wouldn't be jealous, would you?"

She lowered the menu and a grin covered her face. "What would you like to eat?" she asked, ignoring his last remark.

The sound of laughter combined with the crash of broken plates and glasses disturbed their silent moment. Every eye in the building turned to see that the waitress had dropped an entire tray, obviously full of dishes and glassware.

"Oh no! Mr. McCormick will definitely be deducting that out of her next paycheck."

"How do you know?" Daryl asked.

"Because I worked here my last two years in high school."

"You are one talented woman. Beauty, brains, and a steady hand," he said with a chuckle.

"You're so funny. Anyway, I've never seen her before," Samantha added as she looked at the frail young woman with a look of concern.

"I'm sorry about the noise. She's new. Poor thing, she's been dropping dishes all day," the waitress bent down and attempted to whisper. "Personally, I really don't think she's going to make it."

"She will. It'll take a bit of practice. Trust me, I know," Samantha added, changing the subject.

"I think I'd like a bowl of broccoli and cheddar soup, with a ham sandwich with provolone and loaded with onions, chips, and a glass of tea. The food smells good," he said. "What are you having, my dear?"

"I deserve a treat. So, I'm having a mini turkey club with mozzarella and a cup of chicken, wild rice, and vegetable soup, and a glass of water."

"I'll be back with your drinks in a few minutes," the waitress responded.

"My, aren't we hungry? I'm going to go broke feeding you," she teased.

"Trust me, I'm good for it," he added.

After placing their order, they conversed non-stop. The noise became louder and louder as people began to gather for the Saturday dinner special.

"Here you go, Samantha," said the waitress, placing the food on the table. "I'm going to leave you two some wet napkins." She placed the packets on the table before turning to Daryl. "Sir, I hope you enjoy it. Be careful. The soup's hot," she said before greeting the elderly couple who had come in.

"Mmm, this is good," said Daryl as he wiped his mouth with a napkin.

"I told you so. This may not be The Crest, but there's some good eating here in Turner," offered Samantha as she tidied up the table, stacking the dishes, placing the silverware in a glass, and placing the trash in a pile.

"You're a woman of your word. Do you always clean the table in restaurants?" he asked.

"No, but this is like home. After working here for over two years, I know what it's like when people leave an absolute mess, and sometimes, they don't even leave a decent tip."

"I see."

The patrons came, ate, and left. Daryl and Samantha, obviously mesmerized with each other, laughed, talked, and sipped from their glasses.

"Can I get you two anything else?" asked the waitress.

"No, I can't eat another bite."

"Neither can I," added Daryl.

"You haven't tried our new dessert. You can't leave without it. It's a chocolate lover's dream," she added.

"Daryl, you've never turned down chocolate before. Are you sure?"

"Positive."

"No thanks, but we'll try it next time," Samantha promised the waitress.

"Okay, next time it is," she said, placing the bill on the edge of the table.

Daryl unsuccessfully tried to retrieve the bill. Samantha immediately scooped it up before the waitress could take a step.

"Thanks for dinner, Samantha," He told her as they stood and headed for the register.

"You're welcome. I'm glad you enjoyed it."

"Will you at least let me take care of the tip? The food and the service were great. The atmosphere was a change from what I'm accustomed to when I travel. Back home, we have some small cafes, too."

"Deal, I'll let you take care of the tip," she agreed.

While Samantha paid the bill, he walked back to the booth to leave a crisp twenty-dollar bill on the table.

"So, what else do y'all do around here for entertainment on a Saturday night?" he asked upon returning to Samantha's side.

"There's not much to do around here. We're family oriented. On Saturday night, we prepare for big Sunday dinners. What do you do in North Carolina on a Saturday night?"

As they exited, they noticed it was misting. Daryl grabbed her hand and they headed for the car chatting as if the sun were shining.

"We live on the outside of town, and believe me, there's plenty to do. I'm five minutes from the college, and those young people keep the city alive."

"You know what, I don't even know where you're from," Samantha said. "Just where in North Carolina are you from?" she asked, sliding in the car.

"I'm from the country," he replied as he held the door and made sure her skirt was inside the car before closing it.

"Oh, you're a country boy," she teased just before he closed the door and darted around to the driver's side. "I never would have guessed it," she mumbled.

As he lowered his body in the seat, he admitted, "My parents have been there for years. There are over six generations of Chase's. Our spread is known for its winery and tobacco."

Samantha's eyes were affixed as she listened to Daryl. The passion she heard confirmed her theory. He was proud of his land.

"Well," Samantha said, looking at him with a blank stare, "what's the name of your town?" She leaned over the gearbox as if nearing him would entice him to answer her.

"I'm from a town called Chaseville," he said, then dropped his head as if he knew what was next.

Samantha's eyes bucked, her mouth popped open, and her pointer finger flew in Daryl's direction. "Are you telling me that you're a member of the Chase family?" she exclaimed as she took a deep breath.

"Just what have you heard about the Chase family?" he asked, looking at her with a solemn face.

"About three years ago, there was a killing on the Chase Farm that made national news. According to reports, the Chase Farm is almost as large as the town of Turner. If I recall correctly, a member of the well-to-do Chase family was accused of murder." She turned in the seat in order to look at him.

Daryl dropped his head and sat in silence for almost a minute.

"What's wrong? Please talk to me," she pleaded.

"I pulled the trigger, and it was four years ago," was his solemn reply.

His jaw tightened and his eyes seemed to darken.

"Daryl, what really happened?" she asked in a sympathetic tone. "The kind gentleman that I know wouldn't harm anyone," she declared.

"I don't want to talk about it. It's taken me almost four years to erase it from my mind, and I refuse to let it spoil our evening," he declared. "I can tell you one thing, all you've heard isn't the truth. I had no choice in the matter," he said as he turned back to look out the window.

"There were just so many rumors going around until I don't know what to do," said Samantha.

"What do you mean, you don't know what to do?"

"My dad will have a stroke. He's already cautious of every man my sisters and I date," she proclaimed.

"Samantha, you know me for me. You know I'm a person of character and integrity. I was younger and rougher back then. The streets of New York had taught me some hard lessons, but I've changed. I wish people would remember Daryl Chase as he is now."

"Daryl, I can't imagine you ever killing anyone. You said you worked in corporate America. What did you do?"

"I worked at a bank for five years. I began as a loan officer and worked my way up to branch manager before becoming bored stiff. The last six years I spent in New York, I worked for a law firm as a private investigator. In my line of business, I came in contact with some pretty rough characters. That was the old me. When I relocated to North Carolina, I was done with all of the mayhem...or so I thought."

"Just what do you mean?"

"Samantha, please trust me," Daryl pleaded. "I'm new and improved," he added jokingly.

"I'm going to trust you. I believe in you, and I know you're a man of integrity."

He reached over and placed a tender kiss on her lips, leaving her gasping for air.

"Daryl, you are too much."

"No, Samantha, you're too much. You've changed my life. I know we were made for each other. Please trust me." He took a deep breath and sat back with his head thrown back. "Well, where can we go to just look at the beautiful scenery?" he said, putting the car in gear and casting his eyes at her.

"There's a place down by the harbor."

"That sounds like the perfect place. We can sit and watch the rain fall."

"Okay, go to the next block and turn left. Then go to the next block and turn left again," she instructed, while looking out the window at the now beautiful afternoon sky.

The rain had stopped, and in just minutes, a rainbow occupied the evening sky.

"This is turning out to be quite an evening."

"I agree," Daryl added as he took a long look at Samantha.

"Daryl, you better look where you're going. Turn right at the next light, and the waterfront is at the end of the street."

"I'm looking at the most beautiful woman in the world."

"Thank you, but I'm going to ask you to look at the road," she teased.

"No, thank you for trusting me and accepting me for who I am," Daryl added as he stopped, put the car in park, and cut the ignition off.

"All I know is that you've been nothing but a gentleman from day one. All I can do is take you at your word. All I ask is that you tell me what really happened."

"Thank you, my dear." He took her hand and brushed the back of it across the front of his lips, before kissing it. "I will real soon. Trust me."

"Since the rain has stopped, let's go for a walk," she suggested.

"No. I just want to sit and look at you. You are absolutely beautiful."

"Thank you."

Daryl shifted in his seat and raised the compartment between the seats. While she looked on, he removed a little black pouch.

"Samantha, when I went back home after seeing your entire neighborhood up in flames, I I realized didn't know what I'd do without you in my life." He paused and looked into the depths of her eyes. "I went home and fell asleep in my car. I was at a dead end. I thought I'd never see you again," he cried.

"Please don't cry." Samantha wiped the tears from his eyes with her fingers.

"I want you to be my wife," said Daryl as he removed the ring from its safe place and slid it on her finger. "Will you marry me, Samantha Renee Sharpe?"

Silence hovered in the air and the birds flew gracefully in plain view as Samantha tried to maintain her composure.

"Yes, yes, yes," she said, then bent over to allow him to kiss her. The connection sent shivers down her spine. "Oh my, this ring is unique."

"This is Grandmother Chase's. I went to her this morning and told her that I wanted to marry you. She went inside her jewelry box and gave me the first ring my grandfather gave her. She said this ring was to be worn by the next Mrs. Daryl Chase."

Through clouded eyes, Samantha held her finger out and looked at the sterling silver ring. The ring was not only a family heirloom, but also her birthstone. The amethyst ring was set in luxurious sterling silver with black roped silver circling the stone.

"Thank you, Daryl. I can't wait to be your wife," Samantha screamed as if she'd just been granted her every wish.

"No, thank you for loving me for me, and not allowing my past to dictate our future. Thank you also for not seeing me as a goldmine."

"I could never use you. You came into my life when I needed and wanted love the most."

"My love for you came out of the blue. It hit me like a cold morning shower. I wasn't looking for love, but I found love when I found you. My grandmother is anxious to meet you. She wants you to have her original wedding set. It's in the safety deposit box at the bank. She called the bank manager to have him open the bank to get it, but unfortunately, the manager is out of town for the weekend."

"She would give me her rings and she's never met me?" Samantha asked with tears in her eyes.

"I've told her all about you."

"Oh my, I'm ready to meet your family."

"Tomorrow is Sunday. Can you miss church?"

"Yes. Oh Lord, I need to tell my family," she screeched, holding her hand out to admire her new precious jewel.

"Let's do it. I hope your dad will soften up."

"I told you that my dad's cool. He's just protective over his girls."

"Samantha, I love you."

"I love you, too, Daryl Chase, and I cannot wait to become Mrs. Daryl Chase." She reached over and rubbed the side of his face with two fingers. "Let's go tell my folks."

"Okay, let's do it."

Daryl put his seatbelt back on and proceeded to drive, following the directions of the GPS. Before he knew it, they were pulling up in the yard, the same yard he left hours ago after getting the cold shoulder from Mr. Robert Sharpe.

"Don't be nervous. My mom will be so excited."

As Daryl took slow steps and deep breaths, he thought about all of the possible things Samantha's dad would say and how he'd actually act.

Samantha rushed inside the house to find her parents on the sofa half asleep and startled by her abrupt entrance. Her father jumped up as if he was ready to go into fight mode.

"What's all the noise for?" he yelled, wrinkles running across his forehead.

Mrs. Sharpe straightened and smoothed down her dress, looked at Samantha, then at Daryl and smiled.

"What is it, baby?" she asked, still smiling.

"Look, Mama. Look, Daddy. I'm getting married," she screamed, while jumping up and down.

Robert Sharpe stood and looked on as if he'd been turned to stone, while the Sharpe women hugged and squealed.

After the initial shock, Mrs. Sharpe said, "Come sit, you two. Are you both sure?"

"Yes, we are," Daryl replied with authority.

"Yes, Mama."

"Mr. Sharpe, I'd like to ask for your daughter's hand in marriage."

Obviously still in shock, Robert Sharpe stood as quiet as cotton hitting carpet. "Samantha, what do you know about this man? You've known him less than a month, and you're talking about marrying him, a total stranger?" He stomped off and paced around in the hall.

"Dear, you stay here. Give me just a minute. Your papa needs time to digest this. Let me talk to him," said Laura Sharpe as she left the couple to console her husband.

"I told you that he wasn't having it."

"Mama knows how to work him. She'll take care of it."

After ten minutes or so, Laura Sharpe returned alone. "Baby, this has to grow on your papa. Give him a day or two; he'll come around. He always does when one of his girls meets someone and starts talking marriage."

"Mrs. Sharpe, I love your daughter and will never hurt her."

"Son, I trust you. It's just going to be an adjustment for her father. Let me see your ring."

Samantha's arm popped out so fast that the movement was all a blur. "Look, it was Daryl's grandmother's. I'll get mine next week. Isn't it lovely?"

"Yes, it is, darling. Are you staying here with us or are you going home?" asked Laura Sharpe as she turned her head to look in the direction her husband had stormed off to just minutes ago.

"No, Mama, I'm going to stay here tonight. We're going to meet Daryl's grandmother in the morning."

"Okay, baby," she replied, now looking at Samantha.

"Well, again, Mrs. Sharpe, it was nice meeting you. Samantha, I'll see you in the morning. I think I'm going to stay at the little inn on the edge of town," Daryl stated as he walked to the foyer. "Samantha, I'll see you around nine, if that's good for you."

"Goodnight, Daryl. Samantha, I'm going on to bed. I need to check on your father. You know how he gets."

"Goodnight and thank you, Mama." Samantha placed a kiss on her mother's cheek.

As Laura Sharpe turned and walked to the back of the house where she dreaded going, she whispered a prayer.

"I'll see you at nine o'clock sharp. Come on, I'll walk you to the door."

"I can't wait, my darling."

The sound of the engine combined with the rustle of the wind caused Samantha to smile. Just the thought of new possibilities flowing through the air made her smile.

*****

"I cannot sleep," purred Samantha as she talked to Daryl on the phone. "I'm so excited about meeting your family. I hope they'll like me."

"Sweetheart, get some rest. I'll see you bright and early. This hotel is not the Suites of Charleston, but it'll do. The one thing that eases my mind is the fact that I'm only minutes away from you. My grandmother already loves you, and I'm sure the rest of my folks will, too," Daryl told her before ending the call.

Samantha drifted off after staring at the curtains she'd purchased for her mother over two years ago. Somehow, she'd not done anything new to her old room in quite some time. Since her mother's retirement, she and her siblings had made sure their mother never wanted for anything. The aroma of sausage stirred her senses, causing her to rush to the tiny bathroom and make herself decent before going to the kitchen.

"Mama, did Daddy say anything else last night?"

"No, baby, he wouldn't say a word. You leave your papa to the good Lord and me. We'll take care of him," Laura assured.

"Mama, I trust you."

"Baby, I need to get dinner on and get ready for church. We're having an usher board meeting right after service, and I want your papa to eat on time."

"You're the best, Mama.

It was nine o'clock sharp, and Daryl was walking up the porch steps of the farmhouse with a bouquet of red roses in a cracked glass vase. After the first tap on the door, it swung open with swiftness.

"Good morning. Oh, thank you for my flowers."

"Good morning, but they're for your mother."

"Oh," was all Samantha said as she extended her hands to receive them.

"By the way, you look pretty. Amethyst is your color."

"Thanks, Daryl." She turned to walk into the dining room, where she placed the flowers in the center of the mahogany table that was already the home of a chocolate cake with caramel icing under a glass globe. "Mama is getting ready for Sunday school. She'll see them when she gets ready to leave. I love amethyst," she commented as she looked at her finger and smiled.

"Are you ready?" asked Daryl.

"Let's ride, baby."

The time flew. The next thing they saw was the sign welcoming them to North Carolina. It seemed like only minutes before they were reading the "Welcome to Chaseville, Population 3,253" sign.

"I'm nervous. What if they think I'm not good enough for you."

"Trust me, that will not be the case."

When Daryl turned on the dirt road and drove under the huge arch with a C on the brick columns at the base of the driveway, Samantha couldn't remain still. The dust that flew from the roadway contained an orange-red tint.

"Grandmother Chase is sitting on the porch, I see. Why did I not know that the entire Chase clan would be here with her?" he asked Samantha as if she knew the answer.

"She looks classy. You didn't tell me the whole family would be here."

Daryl put the car in park and jumped out.

"Samantha, take my hand."

As the plus-size elderly woman stood, the entire group surrounded her like she were a queen. As she extended her puffy hands, her smile widened.

"Welcome to Chaseville, Samantha. Heck, welcome to the family."

The chatter became loud, and the hugs became tight. From one family member to the next, it was as if they all wanted to squeeze the life out of the country girl named Samantha who they'd heard so much about. The grape vineyards were visible on the north and east of the land, while horses and cows covered the south and west.

"Everybody, come on," said Grandmother Chase. "She's here to see me," she teased, then pulled Samantha by the hand and led her to the screened-in porch that stood feet from the huge ranch house.

Low and behold, they were not alone; a trail of at least ten followed. Once inside, Samantha saw a pitcher of ice water, a double glass fountain that contained lemonade on the top and tea on the bottom, as well as a double chocolate candy cake beautifully displayed on a crystal pedestal cake plate.

Soon after they stepped foot in the screened porch, Daryl began making introductions.

"Mom and Dad, this is Samantha. Samantha, these are my parents, Eunice and Daryl Chase."

"Nice to meet you both," she said, while looking at the remarkable resemblance of him and his dad, while he had only one feature of his mother's, which were the high cheekbones. The sound of the cows mooing and the scent of the grapes saturating the air confirmed that this was indeed the country.

"Samantha, Daryl tells me you've accepted his proposal," Grandmother Chase said as the porch got quiet. "Now, I don't know much, but the one thing I know is that you'll be marrying a man that will do what he has to do to take care of family, and you, my dear, are now family," she added before pressing her lips together and sucking in a deep breath. "Come cut the cake, baby," she said, while looking at the woman Daryl had introduced. "When is the wedding date?" she asked.

"Grandmother, we haven't set a date. If I have my way, it will be as soon as possible," Daryl responded, grinning from ear to ear.

"Lord boy, we got to go to Turner, South Carolina? Baby, do you belong to a church?" asked Grandmother Chase.

"Yes, ma'am. I'm a member of Deliverance Tabernacle."

"What about two weeks from now? Can you pull this wedding off? What do you need help with?" asked Eunice Chase.

"My sisters and brothers will help me. I have some money saved up, so I can do it." Samantha smiled and looked at Daryl.

"Baby, you're marrying a Chase. Money's no object. We'll have our cousins cater the meal, and your soon-to-be sister-in-law makes the best cakes for miles around," said Grandmother Chase.

Meanwhile, days later back in Turner

"You know I made a promise to your father that I'd take care of you," said Monroe.

"You have. You've made sure I've been to all of my appointments, eaten properly, and you've even kept my house spotless."

"I promised your dad I'd do it," he remarked. "Sheretta, I want to take you for a ride, if you feel up to it." Monroe walked over to the kitchen window where I stood looking out at the evening sun while sipping warm tea.

"Where do you want to go?" I asked, turning in his direction after placing my teacup in the sink.

"Let's take a ride to Grandma Tate's. We haven't visited her in a while."

"You're right. She came over after church Sunday and stayed quite a while." I used my cane to maneuver my way from the kitchen to the living room. "I'll be ready in about five minutes."

"Sheretta, you're doing much better. You can almost walk without your cane," said Monroe as he smiled at me.

*****

As we walked out to the car, Monroe held my hand.

"Monroe, I think it's time we start looking for another vehicle. I'm always needing a ride to one place or another," I told him, while looking out the window at the scenery.

"Your dad said he'd be back in a few weeks and he was going to take care of that for you."

"I have excellent credit and a good job. I can buy my own car." I looked at him while he looked anywhere but at me.

"Okay, it's up to you. We can go one day next week," he replied as he held up his right hand as if to surrender.

Monroe drove into the yard, blew the horn, and got out to help me up the steep steps of the old wood frame house. The squeak of the screen door was a sure indicator that Grandma Tate was coming out.

"Lord boy, what is all the commotion for?" Grandma Tate teased. "Lord have mercy. Sheretta it's so good to see you out and about." She slapped her hands on her thighs in excitement.

"Grandma Tate, it's good to be out and about," I responded with a smile. "I'm just about ready to get back to work and go back to my normal routine." I added as I sat in the plastic-covered gold chair in the den.

"Well, what did she say, Monroe?" Grandma Tate blurted out. "I'm old. I can't keep waiting around."

I looked from Grandma Tate to Monroe. "What did I say about what?" I asked in a state of total confusion.

Suddenly, Monroe pulled a black velvet box from his pants pocket, bent on one knee, and asked, "Sheretta Latrice Miller, will you be my wife?"

My heart rate increased, my palms became sweaty, and I was rendered speechless for what seemed like a lifetime. I threw my hands up to my mouth and cried tears of joy.

"Yes, Monroe, I'd be honored to be Mrs. Monroe Tate," I squealed, then clapped my hands, wrapped my arms around his neck, and kissed him.

"Boy, you slow. I thought that's what you two came over here for. I just knew you'd already asked her, and y'all were coming to tell me what her answer was," Grandma Tate declared as she hugged us both, almost squeezing the life out of me.

"You were easy. Your dad's gonna be the difficult party," Monroe joked. "But, guess what? I'm in love and nothing can change that."

"I love my ring. It's so big that the diamonds are almost blinding me," I joked, while holding out my hand and looking at the platinum, ¾-carat, Asscher-cut, center stone engagement ring. A halo frame of similar sparkling round accent diamonds surrounded the stone. Accent diamonds lined the ring's shank, giving it the look of elegance.

"This ring is beautiful! Monroe, I'm so happy."

"Sheretta, you've always supported me. It took the fear of losing you to make me step up to the plate and do what I should have done years ago." He took my hand and held on to it for dear life while looking at me as if he had seen an angel.

"Boy, while you standing there looking crazy, you two need to get the calendar. I'm no spring chicken, you know."

"Grandma, if I had my way, we'd get married tomorrow," Monroe said as he turned to look in my eyes.

"Let's do it tonight. I bet you could get a magistrate to perform the ceremony."

"So you want to be a widow real soon?" Monroe asked me.

Grandma Tate and I looked at him like he'd lost his last marble. Before I could utter a word, Grandma Tate spoke.

"You done gone to talking foolish, boy," she said, staring at him. "You've been a police man for years. You've been shot, stabbed, and hit by a car. Now, boy, you know God is taking care of you." Grandma Tate looked at him with a fire in her eyes I'd never seen before. "You just be careful on the job and you'll be alright."

He laughed and said, "Grandma, I'm talking about marrying Sheretta without her dad's permission."

Grandma Tate's petite frame became stiff just before punching him in his arm with such force that she stunned me, and by the look on Monroe's face, he too was in shock. At her age, I was at a loss for words.

"Grandma, that hurt."

"You've forgotten that the power of life and death is in the tongue. Watch what you say," she said just before turning and walking in the direction of the kitchen.

"I'm sorry, Grandma," Monroe yelled.

"You know better than to say anything about your death. You were wrong for that."

"I'm sorry," he confessed. "I'll be back. I better go apologize."

"You better," I told him, then sat on the sofa after picking up a magazine from the coffee table.

Never realizing how tired I was, I curled up on the sofa, pulling Monroe's jacket across my mid-section, and laid on the pillow. Since the accident, a daily nap was now a requirement.

*****

"Monroe, be quiet. She's sleep."

"Yes, ma'am. Didn't you say you wanted me to change the light bulb in my room?"

"I almost forgot. Let me get a bulb. I'll be right back," she said.

Grandma Tate went to the hall closet and returned with a bulb and a new shower curtain still in the original packaging.

"Monroe, please put this up in the guest bathroom. Next month, my house will be full, and I want it to look pretty. You know your aunts will be checking everything out. They're still trying to get me to leave my house and go live with them in their fancy mancy houses," she huffed. "Homecoming comes every year, and you know a Tate never misses a homecoming at Mount Pisgah," she declared.

"Yes, ma'am, you're right," he said. "You do just fine right here. This is your home."

"Thank you, son," she said, patting the very same arm she'd bruised just minutes earlier.

*****

The ride back to my place was wonderful. The evening breeze was just right, and the nap I'd gotten seemed to energize me.

"When we call my father, I'm sure he'll be pleased. He knows you're the man you should be. He might never admit it, but you're just as responsible as he was at your age."

"You think so?" he asked.

"Baby, I know so. I'd love to get married June of next year."

"I'm going to have to wait that long?" he asked, looking bewildered.

"It'll take me a year to plan and pay for the wedding I've dreamed of since I was a little girl." I looked down at my hand and smiled.

"The money is no problem. I've got a hefty nest egg, and you being the penny pincher you are, you probably have more money than I do," he teased.

"I want a wedding like the town of Turner has never seen before. I want something unique. Let's wait until Saturday at the Miller family reunion to share the news."

"That sounds good. I can ask your father for your hand in front of hundreds. That way, him and your brothers can't hurt me." He laughed.

"You know they're not going to bother you...in the presence of others, that is." This time, I laughed. "You know I'm messing with you."

"If you say so."

"Monroe, I want to be married at my grandparents' house in the yard. We can even have the reception in the big red barn," I told him.

"Didn't your grandmother or great-grandmother die in that barn?"

"Yes, but it's time we remove the sad memories that red barn holds. I want my family to remember the happy times on Miller land. The white house, the lake, and the trees will be a beautiful setting."

"That's what I love about you. You always keep things positive." Monroe bent down and kissed me hard. After gasping for breath, all I could say was, "I love you, too, boo."

A few days later...

As the Chase family drove into the parking lot of Deliverance Temple, eyes roamed and whispering began. Not one, not two, but three limousines pulled into the parking lot. The children who'd been eyeing the playground equipment, but who had been detained by their parents, stopped and looked in amazement. Four other black luxury vehicles and a truck with a large catering van followed the family. The black lettering on the silver catering van read *Chase Family Catering, Servicing Families For Over Thirty Years.*

"Wow," said one little boy who'd stopped in his tracks to watch the shiny black limousines.

Several ladies, who were obviously on the prowl, stopped, stared, and smiled as if they had just hit the mega million-dollar lottery. The young men who they were escorting prior to the entourage kept walking. Some even sped up as if they'd never seen the women they were with before.

As a handsome elderly gentleman opened the door to the first limousine, all of the limousine doors were opened in unison, each driver extending their hand to aid the passengers.

"Thank you, Walter," said Grandmother Chase as she stepped out of the first limousine looking like a queen. "Come, Jefferson, I want to see my Daryl and make sure he's alright. I told you that we should have come into town last night."

She smoothed her hand across her hair and looked over at the gentleman who was obviously a Chase born man. He was just as handsome as Daryl.

"Mother, we are over an hour early, and Big Daryl is with your Daryl. He'll be just fine," insisted the middle-aged man, who sported a black suit, a cowboy hat, and Italian leather cowboy boots.

As they walked into Deliverance Temple, young men in tuxedos and young ladies in pretty black dresses greeted them.

"Welcome to the Sharpe Chase ceremony."

"Thank you, my dear. I am Mrs. Chase, Daryl's grand-mother."

"Nice to meet you. Please follow me to the lounge where both families will remain until the ceremony is to begin," said the young lady in her teens.

"Thank you, baby," the Chase matriarch replied as she strutted with pride.

Almost an hour later

As the wedding began, the mood was set and every-thing was absolutely beautiful. The tables were decorated with candles in glass globes, diamond confetti, and fine chocolates. There were so many wedding cakes to choose from that when the time came, one would have to really think. The mementos displayed in the small sanctuary were strategically placed as to give hints of the lives of both the bride and groom.

Monroe, our day will come, I thought as I proceeded into the sanctuary to take my seat.

The music played, while the guests sat in awe as the wedding party prepared for their grand entrance. The ladies were stunning in their custom-made black dresses. Their jewel-ry sparkled, and everything was on target. The gentlemen were handsome to say the least, especially Monroe. Although he'd only met Daryl a couple of times, Monroe agreed to stand in as a groomsman.

Finally, the flower girls were in place.

As the entire room awaited the entrance of the bride, I suddenly became anxious to be Mrs. Monroe Tate. I wondered what my day would be like.

The End

About Casandra

Casandra's life debut began in Bronx, New York on a cold winter morning. It is said that New York is the city that never sleeps, that too can be said about Casandra. She is often busy writing, traveling, reading, cooking, shopping, spending time with family. Her zest for life is endless.

She later moved to Simpson, a small Village in Eastern North Carolina, where she was lovingly raised by her aunt to appreciate the simple things in life. She spent the majority of her summers in New York with her parents, allowing her the opportunity to see the sights that many only read about.

Being an accelerated reader, she began jotting down stories in her early years. Her story writing continued throughout high school and in her young adult life. Not only has she written short stories, she's written stories that have been used in workshops at women's conferences. Her stories are mind stirring, believable and true to life.

Casandra is an active member of "New Vision Writers," which is under the leadership of best-selling Christian Fiction author Jacquelin Thomas. Ms. Thomas is the Mentor and the guide that keeps Casandra on track.

Casandra in an Inspirational Speaker when time permits. When she begins to speak, all the muttering in the audience ends, all eyes are on her. If you've ever been in her presence when she's speaking, you're well aware of the fact that she will captivate you within the first five minutes. Sassy, sharp, fun, unpredictable and knowledgeable are all responses about her from her audiences.

She has never been one to give up, even when the chips were down. She's seen her share of trials and triumphs and appreciates them all. She knows deep down inside, each of them served a dutiful purpose in her life. With the help of God, she's always bounced back stronger and more determined after each trial. She is no stranger to hard work. She is employed full time and is a dedicated employee. Casandra is an active member of several professional and civic organizations. Her tireless efforts in many of the organizations, have allowed her to receive nominations, honors and scholarships both locally and statewide for her efforts.

Casandra enjoys being a mother, grandmother, sister, niece, aunt, cousin, and a special friend to those who know her best. Her tough outer exterior often frightens those who really don't know her. Her friends are often quoted as saying, "her bark is worse than her bite, she just wants to be tough."

She often spends time with local area youth with the hope that she will be able to enrich their lives. Her Village upbringing is instilled in her heart. It is often said, "It takes a village to raise a child." Her personal theory is, "together our children will survive."

Last but not least, Casandra has studied at East Carolina University and Pitt Community College. She strives for excellence in her studies, for that reason, she has taken an educational leave of absence to complete her novels and short stories.

Energetic at heart, she says that age is just a number and she loves to count.

www.casandrabelchertripp.com

Made in the USA
Charleston, SC
19 June 2013